My Phantoms

Gwendoline Riley

GRANTA

Granta Publications, 12 Addison Avenue, London W11 4QR
First published in Great Britain by Granta Books, 2021

A CIP catalogue record for this book
is available from the British Library.

1 3 5 7 9 10 8 6 4 2

ISBN 978 1 78378 326 7
EISBN 978 1 78378 328 1

Typeset in Garamond by M Rules
Printed and bound by CPI Group (UK) Ltd, Croydon, CR0 4YY

I

1

There was 'nothing for him' in England.

'There were no *"Homes for Heroes"*. Oh no. No *"Homes for Heroes"*.'

My grandmother said this indignantly. And if my mother was there, she used to shake her head and join in: 'There was *nothing*, no. *Nothing.*'

They were talking about my grandfather, who had worked in Venezuela after the war. My grandparents lived out there for eight years, in the Shell Oil company camp, on the eastern shore of Lake Maracaibo. Their house – a company house – was a large, well-appointed cabin on stilts.

I remember various souvenirs of their time in 'Ven', dotted around my grandmother's flat. There were maracas in the fruit bowl, and on the mantelpiece over the gas fire, two painted wooden bookends in the shape of men drowsing under sombreros. They sat back to back, with their arms crossed and their faces hidden.

The photo albums lived under the coffee table. Here were pictures of the Colony Club and the tennis courts, of my grandparents' beaming American friends. My grandfather had been the photographer, but the perspective was a shared one, I think, on all of these unexpected things that had been theirs. There were very few pictures of my grandmother. There were pages of shots that were more sky than land: silvery grey but somehow pulsing with glamorous heat.

My mother was born in February 1949, in the Hospital Coromoto. They called her Helen, after my grandfather's mother, but she renamed herself, effectively, when her first attempts to pronounce that name produced instead a proud, high 'He'en!' My grandmother had thrilled to that, taking the fault as an audacity, which had naturally left her helpless. So then Helen was Hen. The resolute Hen. The remarkable Hen.

'I'd get stopped every few yards,' she used to tell me, of their daily trips to the commissary. 'She was just darling. Everybody said so.'

She had been clever, too. My grandmother and my mother were both keen to stress that: how she had always been top of the class. It was in her teens, back in England, that her purchase seemed to slip. Her A levels were a struggle and then she failed the first year of her teaching course very badly. As per my grandmother, again, they had to 'beg, just beg!' for her to be allowed to retake those exams.

For her part, my mother told me she 'just went mad' being away from home, in London, and free to do what she wanted.

'I just went wild, I just went mad,' she said.

And,

'If you can remember the sixties, then you weren't there!'

I don't think anyone really imagined Hen would make a teacher, least of all her. Going to teacher training college was 'just what people did' she used to tell me, indignantly.

She was a secretary. Later she moved back up north and retrained in IT. She worked at Royal Insurance in Liverpool for nearly thirty years, in an ugly building, an assemblage of dirty yellow blocks with arrow-slit windows, which she and her colleagues were encouraged to call 'the Sandcastle'.

2

I can't know what my mother was like at work. It's still hard to imagine or guess. She maintained that she 'hated' her job. 'Everybody hates their job, Bridge,' she used to say, '*Everybody* does.'

Later, after she'd retired, she told me that going into the office used to make her feel sick. 'Absolutely sick to my stomach, yes.' Why? I asked. 'It just wasn't *me*,' she said, frowning.

It was the same with where we lived. That wasn't her, either. She just wasn't a suburbs *person* she used to say, with a shake of her head.

Still – there she was. In the house with the dark bay window, with the hydrangea bush by the bins. That what my mother did or had done was what 'everybody' did or what 'people' did was sovereign; that it was 'normal': she would pronounce that word with urgent emphasis. Other considerations didn't get much room. Her antipathy to her circumstances was no spur to change; I think it was the opposite, in a way, back then.

My mother loved rules. She loved rules and codes and fixed expectations. I want to say – as a dog loves an airborne stick. Here was unleashed purpose. Freedom, of a sort. Here too was the comfort of the crowd, and of joining in. Of not feeling alone and in the wrong.

In conversation – or attempted conversation – her sights seemed set on a similar prize. She enjoyed answering questions when she felt that she had the right answer, an approved answer. I understood that when I was very small, and could provide the prompts accordingly. Then talking to her was like a game, or a rhyme we were saying together.

'You hated being an only child, didn't you?' I might say. And she would say, 'Oh yes, I hated it, yes. And after I had Michelle I knew I *had* to have another baby because I always *vowed* I could never have just one. I think it's cruel to have just one.'

Or, 'What was your school uniform?' I would ask, not for the first time, when I was reading the list of things I needed for mine.

'Well – it was navy blue, the same, and you had a different-coloured tie for each House and I was Windsor, which was yellow ... only we had to wear a hat, and every day I had to run past the orphanage, morning and afternoon, because they used to throw stones and run after you when they saw anyone from the *Grammar*. And one day I lost my hat!'

She painted a beguiling picture, if you were susceptible to that kind of thing: lonely only child; breathless little girl who had to do this and had to do that. I was not susceptible, but then nor did I ever quite feel that I was the intended audience when she took on like this. There was some other figure she'd conceived and was playing to. That's how it felt. Somebody beyond our life.

If my questions were more than a feed, or if I pressed a point, then my mother quickly got upset. She used to clam up, as if she'd detected she was being duped, or being lured into a trap. 'What's it to you?' she used to say, or, 'Why are you so fascinated?' Sometimes she'd just put her arms over her head and stay still, as if, as in the playground game, she understood that being a statue put her beyond reach.

She didn't just do that with me. My mother seemed braced against an interrogation wherever we went. A hello from a neighbour seemed to both affront and frighten her. The mildest enquiry from a check-out girl was met with terrible suspicion. I used to watch her strand herself – herself and her interlocutor – with her desperation to make it stop. She over-enunciated, cut people off to agree with them. Again, as if the whole thing were a test: a malicious test, on which such self as she had was staked, and which she could not therefore submit to.

The risk of that kind of ambush was also the reason she could never stand going to the cinema or the theatre. She'd always 'hated' it when a man had taken her to see a film when she was younger, she told me. And when I asked her why, she said, 'That dreadful moment when you come out, when you're supposed to say *what you thought*. You walk out in this dreadful silence and then someone has to say, "Well, what did you think?" Just *so* embarrassing.'

This was something she was happy to relate. In her scheme it was a 'right' answer; a secure position. Again, her refusal was proof of something.

I used to ask her a lot about old boyfriends, and her London life. These questions were all one question, I think: why my father? Why did she marry him?

'It was just what you did,' she used to say, when I came at it directly.

'What you can't understand is the terrible *pressure* there was, on a twenty-six-year-old woman, to get married, to *be* married.'

'Did Grandma pressure you?'

'*Everyone.* Everyone did. That was just how it was, Bridge.'

'And to have children.'

'Yes, you had to have children, yes.'

'You wanted to blend in?'

Here she put her arms over her head. That was enough now.

To admit to what wasn't there would have been to give up her treasure, of course. I understand that now. So instead she guarded that vacancy proudly, and jealously.

'If you *ask* you don't *get*,' she used to say.

And, '*Life*'s not fair. *Life*'s not fair, is it?'

To Michelle she would repeat and repeat, 'I can't hear you when you shout. No, no, I can't hear you when you shout.'

Or else she just used to say: 'Tough titty.'

'It's just tough titty, isn't it?' she'd say.

She threw these formulas out like chaff, whenever she thought one of us was 'getting at her' as she used to put it. There was no way past. No way through. Any challenge could only invigorate the pantomime. My mother would lift her chin. Give nothing up. And whatever we said or asked was not listened to but just – taken. I'd see my pleas sported as trinkets.

'What's that?' she'd say. 'That's a big word, what's that?'

She'd repeat Michelle's questions back to her, all the while looking around, looking incredulous, again, as if she believed she had an audience somewhere, and that this kind of swanking would impress them – or him; would mark her out somehow.

Pushing past us into the hallway she would pick up the telephone and say:

'That's it, I'm calling the funny farm. I'm calling the men in white coats to come and get you.'

'I'm calling the Romanian orphanage,' she used to say, to me. 'You look like a Romanian orphan. You should go to the orphanage. Hello? Is that the orphanage?'

I can see her there, in leggings, slippers, T-shirt, happily 'listening' to the reply.

In black leggings, and a Betty Boop T-shirt . . .

The slippers were big, plush novelty slippers, shaped like tiger paws. Or 'tiger feet', as she used to call them, when she sang along to that song in the kitchen: thumbs hooked into an imaginary belt, singing, 'I love my tiger feet!' and trying to get Michelle or me to watch her dance.

Our mother wore her hair in a bob, back then: soaked with mousse after washing, then scrunched like the hairdresser had shown her. I remember her like that, too: sitting in a cleared space on her bed, with her head tipped forward and her hands working away, clutching and unclutching.

When my father died, his sister Mary – his twin – sent me an email. 'Hi Bridge,' she wrote, 'I was very shocked to hear about your dad. I hadn't seen him in a long time but he was my brother and it was a shock. I won't be at the funeral as I don't do "family" these days (not for eight years this Christmas, which I recommend!) but I shall think of you both. I hope you are thriving. Best wishes to you.'

I replied to say that I hadn't seen him in years either, and nor would I be at the funeral, although I didn't know what Michelle had decided.

'Re: the funeral,' Mary wrote, 'I think you're wise. I know it's traditional to share memories at these times so how's this. As Lee was the boy (I was the oldest as you know) he was given the house key when our Mum (your Nana) started work, and after school he used to run home, to get in the house and lock me out. So I had to do my homework on the step (or walk to our Granny Walsh's if it was raining or cold). Went on for years. Says it all and he didn't change. Best wishes to you.'

I was twenty-six then. For eight years I'd been living in London, for six of them in a small flat in Kilburn, with my boyfriend, John. The news about my father was a shock to me, too. I remember the phone call, as John and I were walking up to the station, and how I knew something serious – something bad – must have happened when I saw Michelle's name.

Trying to think about my father now is difficult.

Which thread should I pull?

His being a twin, for instance ... It strikes me now that that might have had something to do with the way he was. And from such a large family, too. You can see why he might have wanted to set himself apart. But his was a funny kind of distinction, wasn't it? Demanding these pointless tributes left and right. Even when he picked us up, for his Saturday 'access' visits. He refused to ring the doorbell. He wouldn't get out of his car. So one of us always used to have to stand by the window, on lookout. Or anyway, that was what we ended up doing. He'd start sounding his horn otherwise, if Michelle and I weren't out immediately and hurrying down the path.

'There's no point in provoking him, is there?' our mother used to say.

Mary had confided that story about the homework before, more than once, including a detail she left out of the email, but which seems characteristic to me. While she tried to get on with her work, he would lean out of the bathroom window to shout and wave at her. He wouldn't have been taunting her then, I'm sure, or not exclusively anyway, so much as wanting her to celebrate his accomplishment with him. My father saw himself as a sort of beloved outlaw; an admired one-off. He felt himself to be at large in a world which got as much of a kick out of him – out of him-being-him – as he did.

That outlaw's camp was what Michelle and I were bundled into when we got into his car. A rough-and-tumble territory where saying hello was a discardable courtesy, for a start. Instead our father would open with 'Lock!' even as we were pushing the locks down, and then 'Seat belt!' as we were pulling on our seat belts. If the weather looked cold, he might say, 'Jumper!', meaning we were to show him that we were wearing one, and if we weren't, by barking the word again – 'Jumper!' – he communicated that we were to go back into the house and get one. 'Haircut!' meant one of us had had a haircut, and would be followed up, as he waited to turn out of our cul-de-sac, with, 'Did they catch whoever did that?' And, 'Hey? Deaf lugs. Did they catch them?'

I remember looking out of that car window. Blank feelings, about home, school, weekends. Here was the golf course. Here were the gasworks. Then the dark minutes under the river. A thudding sound. My father was of a piece with the rest. And his company was something to be weathered, that's all. He had a claim on me – on us – which no one was disputing. Which, in fact, my mother, as was her way, seemed quite excited to uphold. So it was 'Lock!', 'Seat belt!', and then try to let the hours flow by. I'm not sure I even thought of him as a person, really. He was more just this – phenomenon. A gripper of shoulders. A pincher of upper arms. If I was wearing a hat, a snatcher of hats. If I was reading a book, a snatcher of books. Energized bother, in short. And yes, legally mandated.

Unlike my worrying at my mother's psyche, I never had any desire to quiz my father about his life; to interrogate his reasoning. One does come to these peaceful conclusions sometimes. And after all he was no mystery, was he? His nature had to generate satisfaction for itself along the lines I've described. That was it. Getting one over. Being an exceptional case. There was nothing else. With him the difficulty came in dealing with that relentless uniformity of purpose. The way every subject, event or circumstance was used to push towards these same ends. The way his fine musing on his exceptional self did not ever let up. Those Saturdays could feel very cramped as a result.

Apropos London, for instance. Michelle had been on a school trip there with her history class. They'd been to the Tower and the Globe. This information our father attended to as one might a dog's distant barking, before telling us that when *he* first moved down there, he used to spend every week-day evening in an Earl's Court pub called the Coopers, which was a 'den of iniquity', but which *he* also called his 'office'. People used to telephone there when they were looking for him, he said, or call in when they needed to see him. The landlady was 'a real old boiler!' he said. But she used to make him chips and egg, which she wouldn't do for anyone else.

I could hardly credit that scene, even aged ten, or eleven: that convivial tableau, with my father blushing at its centre. It sounded like a fantasy of adult life, didn't it? Albeit coming from an adult. Who were all these people, for one thing? And why would they be seeking him out? This was something he'd been impressed by in a television show, wasn't it, or a film? And which he had therefore decided should be his. Or rather, he had decided that it was his. The indulgent community. The local celebrity. I even thought I'd seen that film, up in my room, one Sunday afternoon on BBC2.

A lot of what he said inspired the same apprehension: that you were listening to someone else's story, not quite cut to fit. He used to call George Harrison 'my mate George!' This because, he said, the two of them had both gone out with the same girl, and had once run into each other at London Airport, when, quote, George was on his way to India, unquote. That one had a second-hand smell. My father also claimed to have been in borstal as a teenager, for the armed robbery of a postmistress. This was certainly a straight lift, bolstering the buccaneering tendency which he found so stirring when he noted it in himself. Later, when I was apply-ing to universities, he told me that at *his* job interviews he always put his feet up on the desk, lit a cigarette, and asked the panel what they could do for *him*. Was that from the television? I wonder. I'm afraid that one might have been taken from life.

It is strange when somebody talks to you like that. When they're lying, but somehow you're on the spot. Was he trying to impress us? But that could hardly be the case: you couldn't value someone's good opinion while thinking they would buy this kind of crap. And then there was the fact that no one was required to respond to his grandstanding. He didn't notice or care about the absence of questions or comments or of oohs and aahs. I'm not sure he was even interested in our attention qua attention. What Michelle and I – and whichever of his other relatives was about – had to do was be there and be subject to him; we had to not be doing anything else. I'd call that a fit-up job, wouldn't you? And hence that dreadful fixed feeling: that for all that was apparently required of you, you could just as well have been a mannequin. Except, of course, *you couldn't*. A living witness was required for the attitudes of this self-pollinating entity. A living listener was required – and you were it – even as the 'living' element was summarily disregarded.

Nobody ever said anything back. Not once. There were no quibbles, no queries. And so Lee Grant strode untroubled through his subjected realm, where he was, variously, the kindly king and the swashbuckling bandit, the seen-it-all sage and the rude clown, the tender-hearted swain and the blue-eyed boy, and on and on … Exceptional cases, every one.

*

One week, when we got into the car, our father didn't shout 'Lock!' but rather leant back between the seats and, raising his fist slowly, underhand, like celebrating sportsmen do, said, '*Gooooooo* Deggsy!'

Michelle and I were still doing up our seat belts. He seemed to expect us to know who this was, and for us to be as invested in this person's fortunes as he was. We didn't and we weren't, and so we didn't react, although, crucially, we also didn't not react. We did what our instinct told us to do in such moments, which was to sort of fade out of the moment. I found out later that 'Deggsy' was Derek Hatton, a rat-faced local politician, that week acquitted of corruption. For now, in answer to our silence and our bland expressions, our father made his call again, in his darts-referee voice: '*Gooooooo* Deggsy!'

There was still no reaction from us, and our father chuckled when he looked back at the road. What a pair! Not knowing who *Deggsy* was.

That was his opener all day: the pink-knuckled fist raised before him, and '*Gooooooo* Deggsy!' At Mary's house, where we went for our lunch, and then at his mother's house, where we ate our tea. There were no fellow 'Deggsy' enthusiasts forthcoming. Our father was met with the same sort of containment operation Michelle and I had learned to effect: mild smiles while he went on, and then back to what they were doing before. Not that he let that dampen things. Not when he was riding so high. I think he felt 'Deggsy' had scored this point on his behalf, in a way.

*

As far as his own victories went, my father was generous in sharing his methods. Or at least, it made him happy to talk about them; to pass on what small wisdom &c., &c. I remember one afternoon in Tesco, when we were doing his big shop. He was, as usual, making a point of 'testing the produce', that is, pulling lone grapes from bunches which he wasn't going to buy, and eating them, and then taking a large loose tomato and munching on that as we cruised the aisles. This was a habit of his which made Michelle and me, and me especially, very anxious, which naturally only encouraged him.

'I'm testing the produce!' he'd say, proudly. And then he'd try and cajole the pair of us into walking around munching stolen tomatoes too. This was something neither of us could ever be persuaded to do. Our father had an inhibiting effect in general, a deadening effect, really, for all of his large energy, and these specific needlings and exhortations only ever sent me further inwards. In the supermarket, I remember, I used to try to hang back, behind him, or else I'd get suddenly quite absorbed by a display; anything to drift out of a culpable proximity to his witless vaunting.

On the day I'm thinking of, a summer's day, we were dawdling through the freezer section when he spotted a young woman up ahead of us who was wearing a miniskirt, or a short dress, with bare legs. Our father leant forward over the trolley and sped up slightly until we'd nearly caught up with her, at which point he slowed down, and paused, waiting until she was a little way ahead again, before turning to Michelle and me, conspiratorially:

'What you need to do,' he said, 'is look when they've been to the *toilet*. I noticed this when miniskirts were *first* fashionable. When they've been to the toilet they get an imprint of the seat on their legs. You can see it if they've been sitting on a wicker chair as well,' he said, 'or a garden chair, but when they've been to the *toilet* you can see the shape of the toilet seat! *They* don't know it's there. Can you see, there, back of the legs?'

Hotels, too; he got one over on them when he could. He'd once worked on implementing some software, he told us, which enabled hotels to charge customers – 'businessmen' he said – who didn't have the time to check out, by taking their credit card details in advance.

'Once I knew that,' he said, 'I've never checked out again. If they can do that for businessmen they can do that for me, and if they can't then that's *their* problem not mine!'

He welched on his maintenance payments to our mother for years, in a similar spirit. I know that because he used to boast about it. 'They seek me here! They seek me there!' he'd say.

My father so relished his own triumphs – or the triumphs of people he thought were like him, like Derek Hatton – that it followed (I suppose) that he took an equal, or an equivalent, portion of pleasure in other people's failures. Their disappointments, their humiliations. He could never hear enough about the inadequacy of people who weren't him. And as with his boasting about his past, these things didn't need to have actually happened for him to enjoy them. The fact that he enjoyed them somehow brought them into being, with

21

each innocuous piece of news you shared with him some-how always ending up as a perfect illustration of some risible misstep. Between your mouth and his ear the facts got bent backwards. So he was neither a prospector nor a connoisseur of human shortcomings, really, but rather a sort of processing plant which turned all information into the same brand of thrilling treat: that someone had had a knock-back or that someone had looked a fool.

As we paid our calls, to his sisters, his brother, his mother, Michelle and I were encouraged to share our stories for a second or a third time:

'Tell Chrissie what your mother's been up to!' he'd say,

or,

'Michelle's got this dickhead teacher this year! Tell Owen what you said to him!'

When there wasn't much to tell, no matter. He was ready to take the stand, to give his souped-up version, and then to darken his countenance to make a *serious* point about some-one being a 'a *real* creep' or 'a *real* specimen'.

Yes, people were 'specimens', I remember that. And everything they did – their activities, their endeavours, their choices – that was all 'behaviour'. When Michelle started play-ing football, that was 'behaviour', and her joining Greenpeace was somehow 'behaviour' too. 'No one's impressed by your recent behaviour,' he said, which was another of our father's quirks – to speak not just for himself but rather as the voice, the representative, of some austere adjudicating body.

*

On it went. Week after week. Through the Mersey tunnel with his Tom Lehrer tape on loud. And were we listening? Did we get it? He'd rewind it if we didn't!

And who was our mother chasing after now? Hey?

And was our grandmother still obsessed with Margaret Thatcher?

Did she still keep rotten food in the fridge?

As we passed the sign for the urban farm in Prenton he'd lower his window and shout 'Mint sauce!' and try and have us do the same.

4

In the Coopers, in 1966, I see my father standing on his own at the bar. On his own with the pools form or the paper, with a pint of Coke on the go. Or I see him on the Tube, smoking away, and regarding his fellow passengers with a keen and bullish expression.

He didn't do badly, to manage a London job and a flat, a girlfriend then a wife, a family of his own – for a few years anyway. He too was accommodated by 'what people did'. By a confluence, too, perhaps, of his particular way of going on and what was happening at the time. He was a forthright northerner, in the era of Albert Finney and John Lennon. Later he was a sort of king-of-the-castle seventies man.

My mother, I think, would have grinned while he talked. All of that spirited scoffing. That spiteful authority. Getting on the right side of that might have looked like a way in to something, to her.

Their shared accent would have been an attraction, too, for both sides, I'm sure: setting them apart and drawing them together.

All she would have had to fit herself to then was making sure he always felt so puffed up. That would have been something, wouldn't it, for a person without bearings? I even think it might have made her happy – in the moment, anyway – for here was a game which, if she could never quite win, then she could at least keep playing.

Only she lost her balance there too, somehow. It wasn't quite right. Wasn't quite it. She left him after seven years. She snatched her chance, after some kind of scene with her parents. Proudly, she told me how her father and my father had ended up standing in the kitchen, 'jabbing each other in the chest, yes'. 'You don't talk to my daughter like that!' her father had said. And proudly, shyly, she told me how she had been required to choose by her father, there and then, and how she had chosen him, yes.

'There's no point in provoking him, is there?' she used to say – to repeat – chivvying Michelle and me to find our coats and shoes; to be ready ten minutes before our father was due. Even back then I knew that she was talking to herself, really; whisking herself through the task at hand. My mother had her sayings, but she did not give real advice, ever, about anything.

Here, 'There's no point in provoking him, is there?' seemed to mean, 'There's no reason for me to behave in a sane and

civilized way when he doesn't (is there?), not when there's a
golden opportunity here for me to join in and be mad too.'
And she didn't even mean 'provoking', did she? She meant
an omission, not an action. She meant: You mustn't fail to
anticipate something he could plausibly decide to be affronted
by. Which rather left one with nowhere to go. Michelle and
I had never been cheeky or disruptive. We'd been mild and
quiet from the start when he was around, and it made no
difference. Anything could set him off, or not set him off. All
depending on how he wanted to feel; on what kind of satisfaction he wanted to extract. Not provoking him could provoke
him. It often did provoke him. She knew that. Why did she
like to pretend otherwise? For excitement's sake, perhaps? Or
because she didn't want to feel left out? I've an image of a dog
trying to join in with a football match, but that's possibly too
wretched. I think her mental sleight was more akin to the way
Michelle and I, after our swimming lessons, used to hit the
buttons on the arcade games in the snack bar: we hadn't put
any money in, but nonetheless persuaded ourselves that we
were affecting the progress of the yellow lights, which flashed
in steps, then slowly cascaded. In fact, there were a lot of children who liked to do that, as I remember. It must be a thing
children like to pretend. If someone else had got there first, I
used to wait for my turn, not too close to the machines, but
not too far away either.

My mother left my father before I was two. I have no memories of my parents married. I would lay odds, though,

that, with him, she went in for her fair share of provoking. Proactive provoking, I mean. Because she felt neglected and therefore frightened. Perhaps she told herself he'd find it stimulating, a little bit of pertness, a little show of initiative; that it might lead to a chase or a tickle attack, or some pleasure of that nature, of which she might be the rapturous focus. Would my father have obliged? I suspect not. But I can't say that would have put her off. My mother could be dreadfully hard to put off.

When I think of her now, I think that's what I see, or feel, most of all. Her keyed-up look: fixed on something; fastened on something. A horrible persistence. A sort of mulish innocence.

She was mulish, when she wasn't completely biddable, and each mode always at precisely the wrong time. Like a mime's recalcitrant prop: the door that wouldn't give until it did and sent you sprawling.

5

My aunt Liza was not answering her door. Twice my father had pressed the bell. Now he knocked: a smart tattoo with his knuckles.

Her car was there. She knew she was down to feed us.

'We can guess where she is!' he said, to Michelle, with a chuckle.

A few more seconds passed. Now he bashed on the door, with the side of his fist – as if this were a police raid.

'Huh!' my father said, when there was still no sign of life.

He walked down to the end of the driveway and looked up and down the road. On his way back, he walked behind me, and took my book from my coat pocket. I was reading *Villette*, from the school library. He held it up, over my head, at arm's length.

I didn't reach for it, I stood still, but he pushed me away with his free hand anyway, grinning at Michelle all the while. '*Ah ah ah ah ah ah ah*,' he said.

Liza was my father's oldest sister. When she appeared, a few moments later, she said, 'Hello gang!' and then stood aside for us to troop in – my father first. He was following his nose to the kitchen now.

'Are we all on lemmo?' Liza said as we took off our coats and hung them up in the hall. From the kitchen doorway I watched her set out four pint glasses and then add ice and a thick slice of lemon to each one. She filled the glasses from a big bottle of R.Whites.

'*Wuthering Heights*!' my father said. And when I didn't respond, he went on, 'That's your mother's obsession. Is it her making you read that?'

By 'obsession' my father usually meant 'interest', if that, but I'd never heard of my mother having any interest in *Wuthering Heights*.

'No,' I said, 'it's from the library.'

'Your mother's one obsession!' he said. 'I never knew what she was talking about! I learnt *something* about it when the BBC did an adaptation. I only watched from pure curiosity. Liza? Did you see that? It was probably up to the usual standards of an adaptation! But the *impression* it conveyed ... It's really ghastly. Really creepy.'

'It explained a lot,' he said. 'About your mother.'

'Is that her book?' he said.

*

Liza had made her vegetable curry. When we went through and sat down there was a pot of vanilla yogurt on the table, and some green salad, and half a loaf of sliced brown bread.

'Bridget's brought a book to pose with!' my father said, or called out, as she headed back to the kitchen, but if she heard him, Liza did not follow that up. She came back in with a large pan of curry, and then with four plates, warm from the oven.

'Dig in, gang,' she said. 'Don't wait.'

Liza was the first vegetarian I ever met, and a good advert for the regimen: she was friendly and energetic. She was surely one factor in both Michelle and I deciding that we wanted to stop eating meat. Vegetarianism counted as 'behaviour', of course, so my father had some hay to make with that whenever we were at her house. That if we didn't eat cows there'd *be* no cows; that kind of thing. We *wanted* those animals to go extinct, did we? he said. And there were endless remarks about wind. Still, he always tucked into her food. He would even allow that it was tasty, with one caveat: 'Be nicer with some chunks of chicken!' he used to say. And then, stage-whispering to Michelle and me, he might say, 'Don't worry, we'll get some nuggets on the way back!' Liza gave no appearance of not enjoying all this. She ate her food, she smiled at Michelle and me.

'So what's the news, gang?' she'd say.

That afternoon, back at his place, I sat where I always sat, next to him on the settee, by the window. Michelle was in

31

the chair with the footrest, having her own thoughts too, I expect.

He watched the same things every week: football, if Everton were playing, otherwise a Western on Channel 4, then *What the Papers Say*. Then it was time to go to his mother's for our tea.

No football that day. Instead: galloping, whinnying, gunshots. I'd look up from my book when there was a commotion and see a red kerchief or a cloud of creamy dust.

At a certain point, I became aware that my father was up to something to my right. He was sitting up straighter, and I could see Michelle doggedly ignoring some kind of call on her attention. When I turned to look at him he scrambled to hide something, or anyway to perform trying to hide it, and then to perform looking innocent. It was an Argos catalogue, which he'd quickly pushed under a cushion. Evidently he'd been doing some kind of impression of me.

Later, I put together where he'd got that business about *Wuthering Heights*. My mother liked the Kate Bush song, that was all. She'd sing along if that came on, and do a sort of flapping dance, and if Michelle or I were around, would try and get us to look at her dancing. She must have done the same with him, once upon a time. That's what he'd meant by her 'obsession'.

6

There were two books in my father's flat: an old *Private Eye* annual and *The Complete Henry Root Letters*. Both volumes sat gathering dust on his bathroom windowsill. But my father was a reader. He was one and he always had been one, he let me know on the drive over the following week.

'I've got thirty-odd years on *you*,' he said, chuckling.

'If we say we both started *seriously* reading at age *eight*,' he said, putting it together for me, 'then you've got five years and I've got thirty-five years!'

'You do realize that I'm a lot older than you, don't you?' he said, chuckling again.

He continued to muse on this long career as we dipped into the tunnel:

'It is *interesting*,' he said, 'at my age, *re*-reading is a particular pleasure ...'

*

After that, if ever I took a book with me on Saturday, I had to bank on my father snatching it from me at some point. If I were reading on his settee, he might pretend to yawn and stretch, and grab my book. Or on his way back from the kitchen, or the loo, he might walk behind the settee and reach down from above. There was nothing to do but wait then, while he applied himself.

If the writer or the book was one he had heard of he often used to just say, 'Huh!' Almost involuntarily. As if something was repeating on him. Sometimes, too, it was his grim duty to inform me – as one who should really have done her due diligence – that the writer in question had been seen on television by him, by Lee Grant, and deemed a 'creep' or a 'poser'. All I'd had to do was ask. But there it was. On those occasions he would give the book back to me with a pitying frown, it being a meaningless, hollowed-out object now.

If the name was new to him, then he handled the book suspiciously. 'Never heard of them!' he'd say. (His verdict.) And if the book was American, then it was null because it wasn't *Of Mice and Men*. 'Get back to me when you've read *Of Mice and Men*!' he used to say. Or, 'If you were *seriously* interested in that ah, period, then you'd've read *Of Mice and Men*.' Of a Penguin Classic, he'd say, 'Posing!' Or else he would lean in very close and whisper, 'You're *bluffing*!' And here, as with Liza and the chicken chunks, or Mary and the homework, he seemed to expect me to enjoy this too, almost as if it were part of a routine we had going. As if my reading a book in his flat, because it was what I liked to do, and was a way of getting something out of this stolen – or rather, *collected* – time, was in fact some kind of stimulating struggle, laid on for him, by me, to keep his large and restless spirit in good shape. It was the processing-plant effect again.

I did not have any kind of routine going with this person, however. When he spoke I waited for him to stop speaking. When he reminisced about listening to *Of Mice and Men* on the radio when he was a boy, for instance, and how he'd started crying at the end, and how 'your nana *always* remembered how that affected me!', I waited for him to stop reminiscing.

It was striking how proud he was of his strength of feeling. One would often hear how he'd cried at this or been 'devastated' by that. Here was another distinction, I suppose. I suppose somebody – his mother again? – had remarked on it when he was small, and so up he'd stepped to the role of the sensitive one; the feeling-ful one.

Sometimes, while I was reading or otherwise keeping to myself, this tender-hearted person would reach over and pinch me, under the ribs, using his thumb and forefinger. He'd keep his eyes on the television. He'd approximate a confused look when I reacted, and if I didn't react, he'd wait a few seconds and then pinch harder. Or if I stood up to go to the loo, and if I was wearing my tracksuit, he might reach out and yank my trousers down.

That impression of me got frequent outings, too. Once with an up-to-the-minute twist: he'd gone out and bought a copy of *The Satanic Verses*, which was in the news at the time. When we got back to his place, he produced this book, and put his feet up and pretended to concentrate on it, his conception of which activity involved bunching his eyebrows and letting his mouth sag open.

'Have you not brought a book to pose with?' he said, to Michelle, who didn't answer, only shook her head.

'You don't fancy posing like your sister?' he said.

And again, Michelle fixed her eyes on the sky outside, and faded out of the moment, as we'd both learned to do. She smiled mildly.

'Dickhead,' said my father.

In the world as surveyed by him, there was no shortage of 'dickheads!' And then of course there were his 'business-men' – I've mentioned them. A type he called 'females' had a predatory intent – these included his 'well-fed specimens', of whom he was apt to remark, when he spotted one, that he wouldn't want to meet *that* on a dark night, and his 'healthy-looking specimens!' – this indicating a striking cleavage. Sotto voce, in shops or on the street, he would draw my or Michelle's attention to 'healthy-looking specimens'. Also abroad were 'posers!' (like me) and, more exceptionally, and never seen in the wild, '*intelligent* people'. He used to bring news, sometimes, from the latter constituency. The news was generated by himself, but it was an important recourse nonetheless. '*Intelligent* people' were a respected tribe, like his 'businessmen'.

Their expertise was brought to bear when I was reading my

Chekhov, my *Five Plays*. My father had had nothing to say about that book at first; he just tossed it back to me on the settee; tossed it very carelessly, so that it fell on the floor. I even wondered if his interest in my reading hadn't worn itself out. But it wasn't that. It was that he'd decided he'd have to consult on this one. What he'd learned was revealed on the drive home that night.

'You do know there's no *point* reading things in a translation,' he said.

'Because it's not the original language,' he explained. 'It could be anything.'

'*Intelligent* people learn the language if they're really interested,' he said.

'What you're reading could be anything,' he said, again.

I didn't have much to say to this. I looked out of the window, just as Michelle was looking out of her window.

'Hello?' he said.

Then,

'Is somebody sulking back there?' he said, chuckling.

Next came the tunnel. We slowed for the barrier.

'She's sulking!' trilled my father.

I watched the tunnel walls. Then we were out again, in Wallasey. Here was the golf course, and then our old school.

'How's your ring, Bridget?' my father said. 'Is it itchy?'

'I've been meaning to ask you if your worms had come back,' he said.

I had had worms when I was little. It came from not ever washing my hands. He often brought it up.

'I think you need to put some cream on your ring,' he said. 'It must be very itchy.'

'It must be very itchy,' he said, 'from the look on that face.'

'Do you think *Madame*,' he said, speaking in his la-di-da voice now, 'might find some time when she's not posing with Russian books to put some cream on her itchy ring?'

Such was the flailing of Lee Grant. But he couldn't be discouraged. His system ran on whatever it could get or on nothing. The following week he announced that he'd bought tickets for a Chekhov play: for *Three Sisters* at the Everyman. He'd bought two tickets, just for me and him, not for Michelle.

'Well you're not interested are you?' he said.

'I don't know what it is,' Michelle said.

'Well, you're not interested then are you?' he said, sitting back in his chair, pushing his plate away for Mary to get. 'I'm not going to waste a seat on someone too thick to understand it. It isn't a pantomime.'

'If I was going to a pantomime I might take you,' he said.

'But this is *Chekhov*,' he said.

7

The Everyman bar was noisy, and smoky. The stairs were busy. We carried our pints of Coke carefully to our seats.

My father was looking around, assessing the audience. After a moment, he leant in to whisper, out of the side of his mouth,

'Healthy-looking specimen at one o'clock.'

And then, nodding to a man in front of us who was wearing a greasy silk scarf, 'Now that's a very typical *theatre* look, there,' he said. Again, he lowered his voice to pass on this intelligence. 'A very *thethpian* look,' he said.

A few hours later, as we left, he told me about the play, repeating things we'd both read in the programme.

'The thing you have to remember,' he said, 'is Russia is *huge*.'

'It's a really big place,' he said, seriously, almost angrily.

*

Back at his mother's house, he turned around in his chair to tell her all about it, too; to tell her the story while she served up dinner through the hatch.

'I had to stop myself at one point!' he said. 'There's this woman, the brother's wife, and she was such a bitch, so *cruel*, I had to stop myself just standing up and shouting!'

I can see him there. Knife and fork at the ready. All innocence. All enthusiasm.

That Russia was 'huge' became one of a handful of facts or commonplaces with which our father liked to barrack Michelle and me. It sat alongside rabbits-from-the-hat like 'tomatoes are a *fruit*!' and that the composer Verdi – Giuseppe Verdi – was 'called', in English, 'Joe Green!' That '*really* intelligent people don't go to university,' was one, and, more unexpectedly, that, 'of course, maths is really philosophy, if you take it far enough'. This was a pearl he regularly encouraged us both to share with our maths teachers, with the idea being, I think, that we were then to report back to him on the mind-blown admiration it had drawn.

I wish things had ended there, with Chekhov. They didn't. The following week, instead of heading to Nana Grant's at five o'clock, Michelle and I were back at the Everyman, sitting with our father in the Bistro, with heaped plates from the canteen buffet and pints of Coke. Our father hadn't given a reason for this excursion. He'd only said, 'Change of plan!' And then, though we hadn't followed that up, he'd said,

'You'll see!' and, tapping the side of his nose, he'd said, '*Ah ah ah ah ah ah ah.*'

I liked it there, though, down in the basement. I'd never eaten anywhere like that before: a loud, grown-up place, with garlicky smells and cigarette smoke; with confident conversation, friendly laughter, and wine drunk casually from small glass tumblers.

In the toilets there were old theatre posters pasted over each other on the walls and doors.

One of the girls behind the bar had pink hair in a plush bouffant.

The food was all new to me, too. Pasta twirls with chilli bits and wrinkly black olives (instead of Dolmio sauce) and a little fluted tureen of hummus, and some sort of broccoli bake, all dished out on the same plate, like school dinners – in that one respect. The people standing at the bar wore overcoats and boots and their long hair was crimped or teased, like the stars of certain films or pop videos I'd seen. My father kept saying 'Student!' as if it were a game to identify them. As if he were calling out 'Snap!' He said it when you were in the middle of a sentence, after he'd asked you a question.

We were sitting at the end of one of the long communal benches. While we ate, my father kept looking over my shoulder, moving his head, half standing up. He was trying to catch sight of the entrance, I realized. And then suddenly, hands on the table, he stood.

Michelle could see where he'd gone from where she was sitting, but I couldn't. I turned to look. I saw him reach the bar and take his place next to a woman who was also waiting to be served. She was leaning on her forearms, and had dropped her head, looking towards where the barmaid was. She was one of the actresses from last week, I realized, catching her profile: younger looking; shorter looking, with tatty blonde hair instead of a heavy plait, but certainly her. What was he going to do? What was he going to tell her? I didn't like to think what might be coming next, all because of a book I'd read.

My father did not turn to look at her when he – evidently – said something aimed at her. He'd startled her, I could see that. She looked confounded by whatever he had said: likely some jab about the play, which, if she didn't 'get' the first time, he'd have just kept repeating at her. Something like, let's say, 'Where're your books?' Now she faced him. She wasn't saying much. She listened to him with a bland expression while reaching one hand across the bar and flickering her fingers for the pink-haired barmaid's attention.

My father pointed over at us, and she turned to look, too. There it was. Now we were in play. I went back to my food: a few last twists of pasta, which I had a mouthful of when he came back with this actress, who could hardly say no to meeting two girls who loved theatre, or loved her (or whatever he'd told her). She had her arms crossed, and had wisely left her bottle of water on the bar, to be returned to.

'I had to stop myself standing up and shouting!' my father was saying as they reached our table, and then he looked at her and smiled proudly, as if he were to be wondered at for his unique sensitivity, for his strength of feeling, and for this feat of self-control: not to have stood up and shouted during a play.

She smiled at Michelle and me. She was ready to be friendly to the children. Then she was ready to leave. She was wearing a floral dress, and trainers, and a big bobbly cardigan. Her legs were stocky and glossy.

'Look who I've found!' my father said, to me. Then, 'Don't recognize her?'

'She doesn't recognize you!' he said.

'You saw her last week,' he said. And then, taking hold of my shoulder, 'My daughter's the world's expert on Chekhov.'

'Oh,' the actress said. 'Is that so?' Her accent was different. Irish? (Northern Irish, I read later. Her name was Patricia Sweeney. I found her entry in the programme when I got home.)

I didn't know how to speak to strangers back then. I just shook my head.

'And you do drama, don't you, at school?' he said to Michelle, who said, 'Yeah.'

It seemed Patricia Sweeney should be excited to meet us, rather than the other way around. Which was doubly odd, because nobody was being met, really. No, the whole encounter – this coup – only meant anything because of how it might be brought out of the trophy cabinet later on. He would enjoy telling his sisters and his mother about this.

'It was her first time in a theatre last week,' my father said, giving my shoulder a shake. (This wasn't true.)

'Now we want to see backstage,' he said. 'They'd love to see a dressing room. They're dead keen.'

Again, Patricia Sweeney was taken by surprise.

'Well, a dressing room, I mean, it's quite busy back there when there's a production on! A lot of people working. Did you know the Everyman do tours that you can book? I hear they're great. You learn about the history of the theatre and you can have a go with the costumes and some of the effects and so on.'

Here she smiled at Michelle and me. Lifted her eyebrows. I'm afraid I couldn't respond. My father, meanwhile, was sucking his teeth.

'I only have them very rarely,' he said. 'They're dead keen.'

She looked over at us again.

'OK. Let me go and check. Lee, is it? I may be able to take you through for five minutes. I'll see how it's looking.'

And she was off, stopping to collect her bottle and her glass of ice from the bar and to mouth a thank you to the barmaid.

'Get your coats on,' my father said, and we retrieved our damp ski coats from under the benches while he found his and zipped it up. We didn't wait there for Patricia Sweeney to check what she needed to and come back for us but left our drinks and hurried to follow our father, who was already following her, out of the door she'd just left by, and up the stairs and past the box office, where a door marked Private swung closed behind her. We all waited by that door. My father stood with his chin up and his eyes narrowed.

A few minutes later she came back and did what he'd wanted. She said, 'Ah. You're here.' And then, 'OK, come on through,' and, 'Mind that cable.'

It was crowded in her dressing room with four of us, and three of us in big padded coats, sticking together by the door. Eventually Michelle moved further into the room and I followed. There were two chairs, in front of a long mirror with light bulbs around it, just like in films.

'So I share with Marie,' Patricia Sweeney said, 'that is Olga, if you remember?' She said this to me, and I looked back blankly.

She sat down in her chair and pulled off her trainers, revealing little white socks with dirty soles. She unscrewed her water and poured some out. Then she took the lime wedge and squeezed it.

There was a full Marks & Spencer shopping bag on the other chair. I could see a bag of posh crisps, and a bunch of black grapes in glinting cellophane. And hummus, which was what we'd just had downstairs, I realized, pleased to put the two together.

I didn't say anything and nor did Michelle.

'As you can see, there's a lot of hair pins involved,' Patricia Sweeney said, talking to me in the mirror. There was a Tupperware box full of them in front of her, which she shook and rattled with her free hand, before stroking her fingers through the mixture.

'And there, if you turn around ...'

I turned and found a rail of blouses and long skirts, and a black dress on a mannequin. On a shelf were two dented polystyrene heads wearing wigs.

Our father didn't say anything either. Didn't ask any questions. There was nothing he wanted to know. He was standing very still as she explained the tannoy system to Michelle and me and told us that the noises we could hear outside – coordinating shouts and trundles – were the stage being 'reset'. Finally she got Michelle to pass her a cigarette from her coat pocket. Hers was a heavy brown herringbone overcoat, hanging on the back wall. Patricia Sweeney caught my father's eye in the mirror as she lit her cigarette, before smiling blandly again.

'So. That's that. Can you find your way back, Lee, or will I walk you?'

'Find our way, yeah,' he said, and he stretched out his jaw and walked out.

By the following week he was boasting about his 'private tour'.

Soon enough 'My mate Pat' was enlisted in his retinue.

Two or three years later, his interest flared again, when she started to appear on television:

'Did you see my mate Pat's shown up in *EastEnders* now?' he said one week.

'Playing an old boot!'

'Days of the Chekhov classics long behind *her* then!' he said.

But I was nearly sixteen. The end was in sight. I paid him almost no heed at all.

II

1

My grandmother – my mother's mother – wrote to me several times in my first term at university. She made some flattering assumptions about how I was doing. 'I expect you've met a lot of new people,' she wrote. 'You must be out every night!' and, 'Have you been "up West" yet? (Note the London lingo!)' 'Don't bother about replying!' she wrote.

Strange artefact: a Polaroid picture of me sitting next to her bed in Clatterbridge Hospital. It was just after my final exams, so I was twenty-one. There I am, in my old charity shop overcoat, with my bag on my knee. She has a black eye: she hit the corner of the kitchen table when she collapsed. She's beaming at the camera, though, really beaming.

After my grandmother died, my mother moved decisively. She sold our house and my grandmother's house; she bought a flat in Liverpool city centre, in the Georgian Quarter. It looked rather stylish in the estate agent's photographs which she emailed to me.

I never visited. I didn't see much of her over those next ten years. We spoke now and then. I called her when I remembered. She used to send e-cards, at Christmas and birthdays, these often with cartoon animals on them, which she would then deride in her message. 'Cute, eh?' she wrote. 'Not.'

One Christmas, referring to an animated puppy, she wrote, 'Puke.':

Puke.
From Mum xxx

2

My mother had no friends when I was small. There were no phone calls or evenings out; no visitors to the house except my grandmother, who came every couple of weeks to tidy up and clean.

In the evenings, I remember my mother dancing in the kitchen while she waited for the microwave to ping or the kettle to boil. Her dancing style was energetic: somewhere between a Pan's Person, acting out the narrative of a song, and an actor on the classical stage, complete with attitudes and gestures. Sometimes she wanted me to watch her. She'd call me in to see her spinning on the spot like a Temptation or, once, shimmying to 'Big Love' by Fleetwood Mac, before switching her head from side to side to do the call-and-response panting. At other times, if she clocked me in the doorway she'd stop and say, 'What?' or 'What are you gawping at?'

Her lack of human society was something she lamented quite cheerfully. I can see her there: clicking her fingers and doing a shuffling dance to 'Another Saturday Night'.

As with her hating her job, and where we lived; as with her having got married and had children as a sort of high-stakes masquerade, designed to fool all but the One who was meant to see through it: her isolation could only further endorse her self-image. She was the fairy-tale misfit. The changeling. She only had to wait and be brave.

The unhappy forays she had made into the world outside work played into the same romance: her brief membership of an organisation called IVC, for instance, which was 'a social club for graduates and professionals'. She suffered through just two outings with them before cancelling her subscription. There was a pub quiz in Neston, and then a nature walk one Saturday, followed by a pizza. On both occasions she came home proudly shuddering. 'I just looked around the table and thought *No*,' she said, of the pizza experience.

And then one year, at her work's Christmas do, she met Griff Thomas. He was to be her friend. He sat next to her for the meal, and then, as he put it, he 'commandeered' her for the disco. Later he used to claim he'd 'had his eye on her for a while!', for which reason, for thirty-odd years, she called him 'my stalker'. He enjoyed that, and often announced himself that way, too. One year there was a Christmas card signed 'Your Stalker (Griff).'

Griff was gay. He didn't ever have a partner that I know of. I know there was a period later when he answered personal ads in the *Liverpool Echo*. My mother was furious about that. 'Christ knows what they think,' she said, 'when *he* shows up.'

Their friendship was jazz-orientated: his passion. He took my mother with him to jazz nights or festivals. There was one in Wigan, and one down in Fishguard, I remember, called Aberjazz. They'd take turns doing the driving. They sometimes stayed overnight. Did my mother like jazz? She did not. She 'hated' it. A fact which both of them seemed to treasure. 'We know how much your mother likes jazz!' Griff would say while he waited at the bottom of the stairs. Sometimes she 'hated' it; sometimes she refused even to say that, and instead did some hostile preening as she came down. 'I've got no opinion,' she'd say.

He never came further in than our hallway, and she never went to his house. This too was taken as a stamp of the bold eccentricity of their alliance. 'It's mad isn't it?' he said. 'But then we're not quiet-night-in-ers are we Hen?' He lived up at Parkgate. He told her that she wouldn't be able to get past the front door. 'Hen, honestly, it's a mountaineering expedition,' he said. 'I have a little problem with throwing things *away*.' I'd often come out and watch, when my mother was heading out with him. It was rare, it was interesting, to see how she acted around somebody else.

Here, there seemed to be a mutual obliviousness at work. Obliviousness, rather than acceptance or understanding; but it felt congenial enough. He liked to talk and to cackle. She didn't like to talk at all. She went along with things, but did so imperiously, somehow. Her look when he was about brought to mind that of a cat receiving the tribute of its worshippers in ancient Egypt. Or a personage enduring a bumpy ride in a sedan chair. Griff did treat my mother like the object of a one-man cult. He was all wonder. Her every gnomic utterance was highly prized. She scored a great hit once when she did a catchphrase from a TV sketch show that was on back then, which featured a jazz-club MC in his polo neck. After a number, he would take a long, relaxed draw on his cigarette and say, in a smooth, deep voice, 'Nice.' My mother evidently started deploying this in real-life jazz clubs, something which Griff seemed barely able to handle. That became their routine when he dropped her off, too.

'And how was it, Hen?' he'd call from the gate. And she would call back,

'Nice!'

Most of the time she seemed happy to be taking part in this back and forth, but there were occasions when the obligation seemed to agitate her. At those times Griff had to call out his feed line more than once, and she sometimes resisted saying 'Nice' even then, but instead gave him a 'Yes! Fine!' before quickly closing the door.

In the years after her move into town, I often got a 'Yes! Fine!' when I asked my mother how she was. Or sometimes, if she was feeling harassed that day, she might say, 'Fine. Why? How are you?' My asking was a bad habit, really. What she liked to do was tell me what she'd been up to. That's how I should have started: 'Hi Mum, what have you been doing?' or, 'Hi Mum, how busy have you been?' She could have happily answered that. She could have said, 'Very. Yes. Very.'

She was never short of engagements to list. Every weekend was taken up with tours or talks. She was out several nights in the week, too, at art openings or at Wine Circle; at Victorian Society events. I heard the full rundown whenever I called. It was quite a change, for a woman who used to cringe from all human intercourse. 'Maybe you should have a night in?' I said. 'No,' she said. She sold it as her way of making friends: the next stage in a programme of renewal. 'I'm putting myself out there,' she told me. And, 'You've got to be in it to win it!' 'I'm "*pursuing my own interests*",' she said, quoting the advice routinely given for meeting 'like-minded people'.

Based on this new evidence, these interests were, broadly, art and culture. Along with the private views and the minibus tours, she was to be found at live recordings of Radio 4 panel shows and at the film screenings at FACT which had Q&As afterwards. There were festivals in the city, too: Food and Drink, Literature, Comedy, Jazz. She often bought a ticket for every single event.

'I never stop!' she said happily.

I sometimes expressed surprise at the matter of her outings. 'Are you interested in that?' I'd ask, mildly, or, 'Oh, do you like his work?' I'd say, meanly.

But as it turned out, again, she was more than happy to say no. She said it as a person might say 'So there', and I felt myself driven back, then, by her 'No'; by the thrust of that flaming torch.

Once, I remember, she told me she'd been on a coach trip which included Sylvia Plath's grave, up in Hebden Bridge.

'Oh wow,' I said, 'I wouldn't mind going there.'

That drew silence.

'Were there a lot of disciples?' I said. 'Plath obsessives?'

'I don't know,' she said. 'Why?'

And after all, who was I or anyone else to assume she had to be interested in something to designate it an 'interest'? I don't mean that facetiously. I was being pedantic. I was, as she would have put it, 'getting on her case'.

On a good day, I didn't pick; I just said, 'I admire your energy!' And she took that. Or I said, 'Well, I'd best let you get on with it then!' by way of finishing the call.

My mother was never not out now, it seemed. She was never not busy. This was an advance even on my grandmother's determined vivacity. But then my grandmother had lived through a war, hadn't she? She'd had to run with her friends to air raid shelters. You could see why she might have wanted to face life that way. Would she have been warmed by the wilfulness of her bold Hen? And by her iconoclasm, too? The way – as my mother proudly told me – she had more than once answered an enquiry after her thoughts on a new exhibition she was viewing by saying she thought it was 'All crap, yes. All absolute crap.' I wonder. Perhaps she would.

The fabled friends never materialized, but then, that might not have been such a bad outcome. That the people in these tour groups and at those gallery evenings recognized my mother and said hello was probably enough. She was acknowledged and included; she was in the swim. I'm not sure what she would have done with friends. Friends who, one imagines, might have wanted to ask her how she was now and then; who might even have expected her to return the interest. I suppose it had just lodged in her mind that one should have them; that it was 'what people did'. Friendship featured on television, in adverts; groups of laughing women loomed over one in those blown-up photographs on the walls of Caffè Nero, where my mother, if I was ever in a place like that with her, would always ask for 'just normal coffee! Do they do that?'

Griff was still around, of course. He was a reliable fallback for me, too, when, during those phone calls, I was struggling for things to ask my mother. I used to say, 'What's Griff been up to? Any more dates?' or 'Have you been on any excursions with Griff?' I'd ask in a certain spirit, because I thought she enjoyed the opportunity to huff about him. His name could reliably coax some animation and fluency out of her, at any rate. I could feel I'd put a penny in the right slot when she said, 'Oh. *Griff.* Well . . .'

Her stories about him followed a formula. He would have asserted something about himself, and my mother would balk at having been expected to accommodate it.

'Well, he's got a handspan waist, that's the latest,' she told me once.

'What's that mean?' I said.

'He was boasting how he never puts on weight, and how he's always had a handspan waist.'

'I don't know what that is.'

'It's a waist you can put your hands around. Eighteen inches. He's got an eighteen-inch waist apparently.'

'But that's mad. No one's got that.'

'I know.'

'And he's not even slim.'

'I know, Bridget. You try telling him. You try.'

'He's not buying trousers with an eighteen-inch waist, is he?'

'I don't know what he's doing. But he kept going on and on that he had a handspan waist,' she said.

Griff's claims didn't need to be implausible for my mother to feel indignant. I remember one unremarkable revelation before a trip to the Lakes which left her just as wound up.

'Well, *Griff* needs a "proper coffee" every morning now,' she said. 'First I've heard of it.'

'So he had us traipsing around in the rain as he just *can't start the day* without a "proper coffee". Finally we find a Starbucks – that's *not* proper coffee apparently, and all the time I'm thinking, This bus leaves in five minutes, *please*, *please*, hurry up. Finally he finds this other café, orders his latte. Gets this huge pint of warm milk. And I can see the bus by now, and I can see our group all queuing up and getting on. I'm saying, Come on, *please*. And we run for this bus and I just feel sick, completely sick, from all this running on an empty stomach, and then we get there and the driver shakes his head. "No food or drink." So we both say, Oh no, *please* could we have two minutes for him to drink it? "We're leaving now, love," he says. "No food or drink." Everyone else in our party is already on, and staring out at this hold-up. So Griff just takes the lid off this coffee and pours it on the pavement. Not down a grid. Not down a drain. All over the pavement. *So* embarrassing. I mean.'

It was hard to know what to make of these stories; hard to know how to respond, except with the sort of clucking incredulity I thought she might appreciate. She and Griff had been going around together for such a long time by then, and this seemed to be the way things had settled between them. They were a sort of old-style double act, with him the tyrant-acolyte and her in a state of perpetual affront. *He* was this way. *She* was that way. And as he once said, 'Isn't it mad?' I did wonder, though. Did things settle with my mother? The situations she contrived for herself seemed always to start to chafe and pinch sooner or later. They were never quite *it*. And so it seemed to be proving with Griff. Increasingly, when I asked about him, I did not get the showy complaints I was hoping for. Instead I got a queasy feeling, in the pause after I said 'And how's *Griff*?', that I was tactlessly trying to prod her into an old routine; that she didn't want to.

'Everything's "*we*" with him,' she told me once. '"*We* don't like subtitles, do we Hen?" Or "*We* don't do boring, do we Hen?" I want to say "*I'm* not we."'

Elsewhere, she said,

'Oh *Griff*. Well Griff is fine so long as you go along with what *Griff* wants to do, basically. Go where he wants to. Sit where he wants to. On my birthday he kept saying, "This is your night Hen," but it wasn't.'

'And the way he dresses. Christ. If we're going somewhere nice he has to make a point. He says the world has to take him or leave him or it can just "do one" he says.'

'But he was always like that, wasn't he?' I said.

I was still talking brightly, as if all of this were no different from her usual recreational grousing, but in truth she sounded very down.

'I just . . .' she said, 'if I'm seen everywhere with *him* . . . no one's going to approach me, are they? When I'm with him.'

'Can't you avoid him for a bit?' I said.

'Why?' she said. 'What do you mean avoid?'

'Well, what you've just said. If you're worried he's putting people off.'

'I'm not worried. What do you mean?'

'I was responding to what you said. Can't you just see him less, if he's cramping your style? Or do more things on your own?'

'I'm always out on my own,' she said, with a thrust of her torch. 'I'm out on my own ninety-nine per cent of the time.'

'Well that's fine then, isn't it? What's the problem?'

She sighed here, and I could see why. She really couldn't trust me, could she? Either to take her at her word or not to.

'Am I not allowed to say anything?' she said. 'I was *just saying* he's very domineering and everything has to be done his way.'

'Of course,' I said, 'I'm sorry. That's a shame, isn't it, that he's like that.'

'I don't know,' she said.

'Great,' I said.

'He hates you,' she said.

'Oh, really?'

'*Yes*. I told him about your MA and about Michelle's new job and he said, "I hate your kids."'

'That's great,' I said. 'Well done.'

3

Hate hate hate. But my mother didn't hate. It was just a word she used. It was just her announcing-ness. She thought it sounded vital and dashing. She thought it set her apart.

When I was growing up, one of her regular announcements was that Roger McGough, the poet, was her 'ideal man'. When he popped up on the telly, or the radio, she used to say, '*Swoon.*' Or, 'Shush, shush, it's *Roger.*' It was a running gag with Griff, too, how much she loved Roger and how Griff 'couldn't see it'. Griff thought he was a 'hairy article'. Griff said, 'you can keep him'.

The crush seemed reasonable to me. I liked Roger McGough too. We'd read his poem about 'glassrooms' at junior school. I'd seen his picture on book jackets. I liked his quizzical-peaceable-thoughtful manner. And his look, too. His various looks. The beard and the earring. The colourful tank top or scarf. The green-framed oval-shaped glasses and the rat-tail ponytail with a bead on the end. A nice art school overcoat as I thought of it. My mother, I imagined, liked all of this too. His manner. His look. His poems, even. She'd bought *Summer with Monika* and she had *The Mersey Sound* anthology, with the flashes of primary colours on the cover. She knew some lines from, or the gist of some lines from, 'Let Me Die a Youngman's Death' and would recite them with her right hand pressed to her sternum and her left hand held up as if to say 'stop' or 'no more': the same attitude she employed when she was doing her Dusty Springfield impression.

After she moved into town she went to see Roger McGough whenever he was doing a reading or a gig. She went on her own. She described herself as a 'groupie'. In Buxton once, he was standing outside the venue when she arrived. He was apparently alone, under the marquee with his name on it. That was a moment. My mother told me it took her a second to work out what was going on. Who was he smiling at? At *her*? Finally, turning around, she saw a woman taking a photograph of him.

'It was obviously his wife,' my mother said. 'Tall blonde lady.' She had watched the two of them heading off together, arms linked.

'To get a drink or something, I suppose,' my mother said, 'before the show.'

'And I thought,' she said, shyly, 'you know, why can't that be me?'

I didn't have to try too hard then to resist responding with my usual mean reasonableness. I did not say, 'Well, shall we think about why?' I think I said, 'Was it a good night? I've never been to Buxton.'

'Why can't that be me?' Like a girl in a musical, at the front of the stage, about to sing her plaintive theme. And surely someone, the watcher-authority, Him, would decide it was her time soon?

Elsewhere, to rationalize the slights life would keep delivering, my mother used to say, 'I intimidate people. I intimidate men.' Which of course had been Griff's assessment, too, I remembered, back in the jazz club days, of 'our Hen'.

How confounding, then, how extraordinary, that it did happen; that she was picked out and 'approached'. This man 'sidled over', as she put it, at one of her gallery evenings. He was there with a friend.

I only met him once, that second husband. He was called Joe Quinn. We had a strange meal, in Liverpool, where he was introduced coyly as 'my new *friend*, yes'.

He didn't stand up to say hello. He didn't say hello. He said, 'Aye aye!' and followed that with a long sip of Guinness, during which his eyes were trained on the café's back wall.

One thing they had in common was that he'd been in computers too. Although he had his own business now. 'Consultancy!' he said, and that was all he said about that.

That there were no flies on him was what he seemed keenest to convey, and I didn't find that as exciting as my mother appeared to. She looked shy and pleased every time he demonstrated how unillusioned he was; every time he said something cynical. I remember thinking, *he* isn't much like Roger McGough, is he? And I remember thinking, how curious that she couldn't tell the difference between that and *this*. Between wit and coarseness. Sensitivity and boorishness. These were different things, didn't she know? Opposite things. And if she didn't then what had she been playing at, vamping a swoon at Roger McGough for the last fifteen years? Why had she decided to adorn herself with that foible rather than something else? Were these two men's qualities equivalent in her mind?

'So we're all supposed to call you "Doctor" are we?' Joe said, to me.

'No,' I said. 'Why do you say that?'

'Your mother said you're doing a PhD,' he said.

'Oh yes. I don't have it yet, alas! There's a year or so to go. But even when I do . . .'

'Your mother said, we have to call her Doctor.'

'Oh, right. No. I've never said that, Mum!'

'Or else,' he said.

'No,' I said.

'I knew it!' said Joe. 'I thought, fuck off! Seriously? Doctor?'

My mother raised her eyebrows here and looked happy. When he started in on the menu of the café I'd chosen, she did the same.

'Chilli *Sin* Carne!' he said, 'Fuck off!'

The pair of them bonded like that at the art gallery, I expect. He probably said the paintings could fuck off.

Again, my mother moved quickly. She sold her flat and moved in with Joe, into his semi in Woolton. They were together for two years before they separated. She didn't tell me about that at the time. It was months later, when I called, that she said a couple of things that didn't make sense, and I dutifully followed those breadcrumbs to the miserable time she'd had. 'As soon as we were married, you see, he didn't want to go out any more,' she said. 'He had this new iPhone and he was just on that. Didn't want to do anything else.' She said she'd raised the subject with him several times, 'very, you know, mildly, that he never wanted to *do* anything or *go* anywhere. And he just didn't answer. He'd just sort of, you know, sniff or clean his glasses. Because he was *busy* quote unquote and you know how dare I bother him sort of thing. As if he couldn't hear me sort of thing.'

'And I just hated being in the suburbs,' she said, 'they're just not me. Just. Not. Me. So if you're there you at least have to go out, don't you? But whenever I even *mentioned* it, he would just get up and go in the other room.'

'And then *one* night I said, *Well* then, if *you* don't want to go anywhere, then I *might* like to go somewhere, on my own, and I said, *Yes*, I might just have a night out on my own or maybe go abroad on my own, and if he didn't want to, well, tough titty . . .'

It was during this declamation that Joe Quinn had found his voice. My mother said he 'just went mad'. He told her she was welcome to fuck off so long as she didn't come back: 'Whose house is this? Remind me, Helen, oh I beg your pardon, *Hen*? Did you buy this house, *Hen*?'

So she was in Manchester now, renting while she looked for somewhere to buy. Somewhere in the city centre, she said. Joe had said about Liverpool: 'No one will speak to you here so you'd better fuck off.'

She hadn't been in touch with any solicitors, though. She said it was easier just to leave it. After two years of separation they could have a no-fault divorce, if he agreed. If he didn't agree, it would be five years.

'If that's what you think's best,' I said. 'I know nothing about it.'

'Yes, there's no point in provoking him,' she said. 'And anyway, I'm an expert now! At divorce! *Two* husbands. I don't know!'

III

1

I did not visit my mother in Manchester, either. I did not see the 'city centre apartment' she was so proud of. Nor did I call her like I used to. I fell out of the habit. We probably spoke once or twice a year.

At Christmas and on her birthday, I sent a card and a book. The era of the e-card was over. Now my mother sent me text messages. Not often. On my birthday, on Christmas day, and otherwise every few months. Those were announcements, too. Things like: 'Left Wine Circle' or 'In Scotland'. It was hard to know how to reply to an announcement. What seemed to be required was a reaction rather than a response. I tried to provide one each time, but what followed were often only the same kind of stubbed-toe, short-leash exchanges we used to have on the phone. I'd send 'Tell me more!' and hear nothing, or 'Oh no!' and get 'what'. Once she sent, 'Awful haircut ☹'. I called her when I got that one, but she didn't answer.

She was in a bind, I did see that. She had to feel that she was in demand, that people were interested in her – and *faute de mieux*, I did count as people – but somehow, from me, even an acknowledgement of what she'd sent felt like unbearable attention, or scrutiny: me 'getting on her case' again. I remember thinking it would have been better if she'd had a wrong number for me, or if I'd given her a number to a phone I never looked at. She could have safely broadcast to that. That would have felt like a cruel trick to me, but it might have worked better, mightn't it? It might have worked well.

Instead, the years went by. And now my mother was going to be sixty. In the January of that year, she sent me a rare email. The subject line read: 'Big News'. She was coming to London, she said, for her 'big birthday weekend'. There was an itinerary attached and I was welcome to join her for any or all of her 'exciting programme of events'. Did I want to come out for a meal on the Friday? And bring a friend, if I wanted: she'd pay. That 'friend' was interesting. Didn't my mother know I lived with my boyfriend? I must have told her. Was she being coy, then? Either way, I replied – truthfully – that I was busy that night. Saturday was free, if that was any use.

'Good,' she wrote.

When that afternoon came around I duly headed out, with her card and her present in my bag. It was a filthy day. I felt for my mother, traipsing around in that. I felt for her when I spotted her coming over the Millennium Bridge in her waterproof hat and her too-big raincoat, fresh from an hour in the

Tate Modern. She leant into the wind, her hands held out at her sides. The caption might have read 'PERSEVERANCE'.

'What's she here for?' John asked, again, when I got in.

'For her birthday, she says. And mine. I've got this,' I said, and here I held up my card and present: a book I wouldn't read.

After supper, I remember, he and I settled into one of our old, quiet evenings: reading in the back room, with our rescue cat Puss lying on the rug between us. He stretched out, every so often extending his white-bloomered back legs until they shuddered.

'Good boy,' John said. '*Brave* boy.' This because we'd been given to understand that he'd had a bad time before we adopted him.

The following year, my mother wrote again. Now the subject line said: 'Annual Birthday Trip'. Again she asked if I wanted to bring a friend out for dinner. Again I went out to see her on my own. The Troubadour was her suggestion. It was an 'old haunt' she said, from when she was a student. She called it – she said they used to call it – 'the groovy Troub'.

At seven o'clock I pushed open the heavy door. My mother was already there, at a table close to the window. As I said hello and leant down to touch my cold cheek to her cheek, she said,

'It's exactly the same!'

'Is it?' I said, sitting down.

'But, *exactly*,' she said. She gripped the edge of the marble table top and shook her head. 'It's *uncanny*,' she said.

'Was all this here?' I said, by which I meant the bric-a-brac: the shelves of colourful coffee pots behind her, and the toasting forks nailed to the wall, and the old mandolins, which hung from the ceiling like hams in a smokehouse.

'Oh, I don't know. They must have been, yes.'

'Well, it is very groovy. I should have worn my polo neck.'

'Oh, *no*. That's jazz. Aran knits. And patched denim. *Everyone* wore patched denim.'

We kept that date for the next few years. In January I would get my email, and then on the evening of her birthday I would wrap up and set off, sometimes feeling equal to the prospect, but sometimes – often – feeling full of apprehension or antagonism. The weather didn't help. Once, having laboured through an exhaust-flavoured squall, I stood wet-legged by our booth, easing off my half-sodden coat, and said,

'Why don't you move your birthday? Like the Queen. You could come down when it's less freezing cold.'

'Oh. No,' my mother said, 'my birthday's today.'

I was stashing my dripping brolly now, then trying to wipe my wet hands on a lot of glossy paper napkins.

'Well, have two!' I said, and I sat down and shivered my shoulders. 'Have two, like the Queen does, that's what I'm saying.'

'What do you mean?' she said.

'You could come down in the summer instead. I'm not

trying to take anything away from you. This would be a bonus. You could spend your February birthday doing something in the warm. In your flat. Michelle could come round or something.'

'I feel an *extra* resentment,' I went on, swiping again at my wet hands and face, 'when I have to come out in the dark and the cold.'

'Oh. Well,' she said. 'Pardon me. Pardon me for . . . being born.'

'Oh come on. Don't you think? It can't be fun walking around in this.'

The waiter arrived then. My mother fixed her eyes on her menu and frowned. Her free hand was tapping on the table.

'Just some fizzy water please, for me,' I said. 'We're still deciding, aren't we, Mum?'

She had to look up then. She said, 'Yes. No. Not yet.'

But after he'd left she dropped her chin again. She looked scolded. I was going to have to coax her out of the corner I'd chased her into.

'Remind me who you used to see here?' I said, brightly.

'Oh,' she said. 'Yes. I don't know. Various people. *Um?* Who did I see?'

It wasn't the first time I'd asked her. But this was a question she seemed to like answering, or rather, it was a subject she seemed to like being quizzed about.

'Not Bob Dylan,' I said.

'*Not* Bob Dylan, no. I would have remembered that!'

'Bert Jansch?'

She frowned again. 'Bert Jansch. Who he?'

'I don't know, but his name is on the wall over there.'

'Is it?' she said, doubtfully. 'I don't remember a Bert Jansch. No.'

'Acker Bilk?' I said.

'Mmm ... No,' she said. 'Bit late for Acker Bilk!'

'But this was the place to be?' I said, brightly.

'Oh yes. Yes. It used to be dead groovy,' she said.

'Yes, they used to call it "the groovy Troub",' she said, holding on to the edge of the table again, and smiling around at the room.

Our birthdays were one week apart. I'd always take her a card and a book, and she'd always have brought the same for me. That exchange was easy enough. After that, I asked about her hotel, which was always 'Fine, yes,' and then about the films and exhibitions she was going to see. She was happy to list them, if not to talk about them. If there was something going on in the news, I could try that, but there too she would resist being put on the spot, and sometimes, as when I was little, she simply didn't reply at all. She only smiled and stayed very still, or else just said, 'Yes, yes' or 'I know, yes,' while straightening her cutlery. And then she was back to looking at me, waiting happily for my next gambit.

Which might be ... life in Manchester: how was that? Her 'social whirl' as she called it. 'Fine, yes,' she would say, quickly, smiling, because she had the right answer, she'd met that play. So then I might try asking whether she had seen or done anything lately that had been *particularly* good. In answer to that I would get another list. Everything she'd seen or done. That all sounded like the pre-Joe Liverpool scene, more or less – festivals, openings, jazz – but with some volunteering now, too, now that she was retired.

Was that interesting? I asked.

'God, no,' she said, 'dead boring.'

'How's that?'

'It just is,' she said. 'You stuff envelopes for four hours, and they give you two biscuits. It's slave labour!' she said. 'It is! You always read Oh, volunteer and meet new people, meet like-minded people, but there's no one you'd want to meet, really.'

'Oh dear. Weirdos?'

'Mmm . . . sort of "eccentrics". You can see why they don't have friends. I mean, you can see why they're volunteering.'

'So are you going to stop that?'

'Oh no,' she said.

I think she liked finding life a little bit crap. It encouraged her, in a way. 'Boring' films, 'crap' exhibitions, 'mad' people, these she could happily talk about. This was a world she could be part of. And events that had gone wrong: they were a boon, too. One year, she'd been to a lecture where a microphone had failed to work. That cheered her up no end. 'Talk about *It'll be Alright on the Night*,' she said. 'Everyone was shouting, "Speak up." And this poor man was going bright red!'

It hit a sweet spot, an experience like that.

I tried to keep the conversation focused on her. I was warm.

I was engaged. I acted impressed or shook my head and commiserated, where appropriate. When she remembered her cue and asked me her own set of questions I was friendly, I hope, but I didn't volunteer too much. I didn't, as a rule, talk to her about anything that mattered to me. Why upset her by talking about things she couldn't understand or enjoy? And nor did I want to feel stupid myself. It was no fun to ask in good faith, 'Do you know what I mean?' and have her say, 'Oh yes, definitely, yes,' and then grin and shake her head. That brought a flush of shame. Which is what you will get, of course, if you behave as if things are other than they are.

Accounts of my own minor upsets or embarrassments generally went down well. Coffee spilled on new trousers. A missed train. That kind of thing.

'Oh don't Bridge, don't!' she would say happily, then. And, 'Stop! Stop!'

I remember once she said, 'Stop, Bridge! No! I can't bear disappointment!'

She liked farcical situations. Near misses or terrible coincidences. I provided them, too; sometimes wholly invented them. Things like: the friend I lived with had bought tickets to a concert. They'd been delivered next door by mistake. It *just so happened* that our neighbour had it in for us because one night my friend had banged on the wall for him to turn his Playstation down. We realized one of us was going to have to knock on his door to get the tickets! My mother loved that. It had never happened. But she was able, then, to shake her head and say, 'No!' or, 'Stop, Bridge, I can't bear it!'

Conversely, if I let slip about anything lucky, or nice, in my life, that could be tricky. Once, when I mentioned that I'd been to a Christmas party, she looked very hurt.

'You've just told me about all sorts of festive drinks dos,' I said. 'This was just like them.'

She wasn't convinced, though. When I didn't tell her enough about it, she said,

'Oh tell me. Oh let me live vicariously, Bridge!'

'There's nothing else to tell!' I said, and I searched my memory for a detail I could share.

'I got stuck with a really boring woman for about ten minutes,' I said.

'Oh no!' my mother said.

'So typical,' I said, 'in a room full of interesting people.'

That was a slip-up. I knew it as soon as I'd said it.

'Mmm,' she said, bravely.

I tried to get her back: 'The dreadful thing is, I think she felt she'd got stuck with me, too! But neither of us had the wherewithal to break it off.'

'Aargh!' said my mother.

And encouraged, I went on, 'I think it's worse when you feel you're the boring one!' I said. But there again, that was wrong: I'd given the impression now of such a party-rich life that I could make generalizations.

'Mmm,' she said, again. And then, again, she smiled bravely and looked at me expectantly. What to say? What else was there?

'Shall we have a cocktail, Mum?'

'Coo!' she said.

'A birthday cocktail,' I said.

That was the way. Keep shovelling in the bright friendliness; the treats. Things that had happened and things that had not. Keep shovelling it all in.

That scrabble for combustible material ... My instinct was that it was the best thing to do; that it kept something else at bay. But I did not feel good about it; about the way, for instance, I used to ask this routinely overlooked and ignored woman about men. 'Any potential new boyfriends?' I'd say, brightly, every year, knowing that that would take care of half an hour or so as my mother talked up her latest crush and I reacted and speculated, and asked for details, and made a show of considering what they might indicate. I remember there was Simon in Wine Circle one year, and then a man who had given a speech on the renovations at Central Library. There was Ponytail Ed: a local tour guide who always said hello, and the next year a man she'd seen on his own in Pizza Express when *she* was on her own in there, too. Having listened to her pen portraits, her 'picture the scene' descriptions of these encounters or sightings, it would fall to me to be encouraging or sceptical. I tended to the latter, which she seemed to enjoy.

What was my justification for this charade? That we were playing pretend together, maybe?

Talking about men was 'what people did', of course; what girls on a girls' night out did, while sharing a bottle of wine.

Tinnily clucking and coo-ing with her, I used to say, 'Mum, you're incorrigible!' and she seemed to like that, very much, for a few moments, anyway, before that expectant look came back and I had to think of something else to ask or say. Something else in the same line. It was all wrong though, and the price I paid for that – for all that lavishing of admiring incredulity – was that sometimes a suspicion would creep in, as I winced at her description of Simon's jumpers, or wondered how 'we' could track down a man who'd picked up the purse she had dropped on Market Street: a suspicion that her poor heart was lighting on a new object as we spoke, and that that object was – of all things – *me*. Or me in the role of indulgent best friend, anyway; me as a confidante from central casting. I'd feel sure I could see that happening. And what then? Any idea that the two of us were indulging in a bit of joint make-believe was gone. And again, I would feel ashamed, and grubby, and low. I would have to try to ignore her look of shock and betrayal as I stepped neatly out of character; as the illusion I'd raised disappeared. She would need distracting then, and quickly. With another birthday cocktail. Or with a question about Griff, or Michelle. Or about her *not* having seen Bob Dylan.

But then, even when I was being straightforward with my mother, acting in good faith, or at least better faith, my efforts seemed to run aground on that same shoal. I could distract her, but that seemed to be all I could do. She did not seem able to accrue any fellowship or absorb any solace. I was filling a cup that had a hole in it, really, and so, because

I couldn't distract her completely and for ever, those evenings often ended in upset: that this was all she was getting; which is to say, in the absence of permanent distraction: nothing.

It hurt me, too, to have it all valued at nought. Again, I could drop my smile quite suddenly, seeing that. I could snatch back the smile, and the rest, as any fraught child might be moved to repossess an unappreciated gift.

I grew to dread those meetings. From which I would come home contrite.

When I was in my twenties, if anybody asked about my parents – as older people often did – my aggressive little offhand chronicle would land with this:

'My mother's had *two* terrible husbands, yes. She's on the lookout for a third.'

I must have been rather pleased with that. I must have thought that rather sophisticated. I would keep wheeling it out.

'My mother's had two dreadful husbands, yes. She's doing her best to land a third.'

'She's scouring Greater Manchester for a third.'

Never mind my making anyone listen to that; it wasn't accurate, or honest. Whatever it was she wanted, my mother had never scoured anywhere. She was what she said she was: 'out there', 'in it'. Relentlessly in it.

Nor was that in the service of finding a husband, really. I knew that. Or not a husband qua husband, anyway. Qua what, was the question. What would a husband have looked like a way in to? Not life. She didn't want that. Perhaps some private billet in life. A place she could feel was her rightful place, from where she could look out at other people less fearfully. That doesn't sound so outlandish, does it? The trouble is, I think being let in to that place was meant to be it. To be recognized, welcomed, delivered . . . This was the model of so many of the situations my mother contrived for herself and then extolled. Her social whirl. Her house moves. Her holidays, later. But they never were 'it'. The inclusion would turn to exclusion, every time.

Here was that mulish innocence, again. And at the nub of it, still, that expectant look. How could she look like that, given what she'd got so far? Was she immune to what happened to her? And if she was, how could her expectation ever be met? It couldn't, could it? Expectation was the point. She would have to stay that way: hopeful, eager, and absolutely unreceptive.

That was why she suffered, I think. And that was why I started to feel so wound up, walking up from Earl's Court every February the thirteenth; walking through the wet wind, with every step generating more resentment and fear, which then whirled around my chest as in a turbine. I knew what I was about to step into when I pushed open that black door: a zone charged with that snatching dissonance.

My mother was always there when I arrived: smiling at the room; determined to get the most out of her evening.

'Hi Mum!' I'd say, leaning down to touch her shoulder and kiss her cheek. 'How are you?'

And lifting her chin, she might say, 'Fine, yes!' or sometimes, 'Fine, yes! Very!'

2

After five years in the Troubadour, I suggested a change. A new venue might give my mother and me more to talk about; different surroundings could spark some conversation. Perhaps, too, it might help her to feel less excluded, if I took her somewhere I liked. I told her to meet me in a pub behind Piccadilly and from there we walked round together to have lunch in a new vegan café in Crown Passage: a place, I said, that I often went to with a colleague after our Friday seminar. That was another lie – we'd been once – but when I told her that she said, 'Coo!' and she feigned some nervousness.

The café was in a basement, underneath a closed sandwich shop. We took a table near the back, hung our coats on the wooden pegs behind us, and smiled as we shuffled our chairs into place. It was a peaceful little nook: not too busy on a

Saturday. It felt like a nice, freshly whitewashed burrow. I might have said that if I'd been with anyone else.

My mother made a show of her confusion with the menu, just as she used to do in coffee shops.

'I don't know what anything is!' she said. And, 'Help!'

But she made a show of how game she was, too, and smiled and said, 'Same, yes' after I'd ordered: same food, same drink.

'Are you sure?' I said. And with some dash, she said, 'In for a penny!'

When our drinks arrived – white wine in little French tumblers – I lifted my glass and said, 'Well, cheers, Mum. Happy birthday.'

'Oh. Yes. *Cheers*,' my mother said.

We both sipped our wine. I smiled and looked around. At the table next door but one a couple were leaning back as their plates arrived, heaped with some kind of stir-fry. I raised my eyebrows at my mother, who grinned back nervously.

'Well I think your hair looks nice,' I said. This after that unhappy text a few weeks back.

'Oh,' she said, and immediately put her right hand up to her head.

'Yes. That was a whole . . . *saga*.'

'What happened?'

'*Well*,' she said. She'd been for this expensive haircut, she said, after reading a profile of this stylist in the MEN.

'Anthony made "everyone feel special" it said. Well. Not me. *No*. Anthony did not make me feel special.'

'Oh no. Really?'

'Well basically he just kept going on about the lady he'd seen *before* me, who apparently was some famous TV presenter, but I'd never heard of her.'

'Oh dear.'

'As soon as he appeared he said, "*Now*, do you know" – well, whatever her name was, and I said No, and that was that really. I was sort of beneath bothering with then. "Oh, she's never heard of" – whoever she was. This was a personal insult, apparently. Anyway, I don't know why he asked because even when I said no he kept going on about her. How *she* had "lovely long hair" and how *she* was in the panto at the Opera House, how *she* came in for a blow dry before she went on the Red Nose Day show, and how *she* was worried he'd be impossible to get a slot with now he was "famous".'

'Oh Christ.'

'I had to listen to him going on and on about this other woman's wonderful hair,' my mother said. 'I mean. Hello? And they'd brought me the world's smallest glass of Prosecco, which was included, you know – sounds nice, but every time I leant forward to sip from it he sort of huffed like I was holding him up or something, and anyway it was so sweet. It just instantly gave me an absolutely splitting head.'

'Oh dear,' I said, again. I didn't have much else to offer. Only, perhaps, some fellowship: that I too knew what it was to be helpless in the hairdresser's chair.

'I don't look forward to appointments,' I said. 'It is stressful. I think they take one look at me and give up. If you don't look like a model, as you say. Some of them.'

'I was there for under an hour,' my mother continued, 'I mean it was wham bam thank you ma'am and don't darken our doors again sort of thing.'

'Christ. And you were hundreds of pounds down?'

'No,' she shook her head, 'not hundreds, but it wasn't cheap. So, just, handing over this money thinking, well, thank you for that. And as for *him*. As for Anthony. I mean he'd looked quite attractive in the article but when he eventually graced us with his presence he was tiny! This tiny little man. Like a little sort of dwarf Richard Gere.'

'Yikes,' I said. 'Was it a young person's place?'

'Oh. I don't think so. But it shouldn't be should it? I mean I should be able to go there. I don't want to be getting a cauliflower perm just yet.'

'No, I didn't mean that. I just mean, was it trendy rather than stylish? That's a better way to put it.'

'Well I don't know,' she said. 'It didn't look young but you never know, do you? The girls were all young with blue hair and piercings but he was my age. He was sixty-odd. But with these, you know, sort of Widow Twankey eyelashes.'

'Your hair looks nice, but it does look the same.'

'It looks exactly the same, *now*. Actually, I think the haircut was probably OK, but the experience was just dreadful. Just awful.'

'Oh God. How horrible.'

'I got home and just sort of sat in the dark.'

'Oh God, don't say that. I feel like writing a complaint.'

'Oh no. No, Bridge. That's just, you know, life as an *older woman*. You've got all that to come, lucky you!'

'Yes. If I'm spared!' I said, and she smiled at that.

'How is Manchester otherwise?' I said. Sitting back. Smiling myself, now.

'*Well*,' she said, 'Manchester. *Hmm . . .*'

And then she said nothing. She shook her head.

'Not good?'

'Oh. Yes, it's fine,' she said, frowning. 'I *love* Manchester.'

'OK.'

'I love Manchester,' she said again, indignantly, 'but what I didn't realize, when I bought that flat, was that I was basically moving into a Chinese hall of residence.'

'Oh lord. Really?'

'Yes *really*. It's dreadful. I mean, the *flat's* nice. I love love love the *flat*, but, you know, you think "city centre apartment", you think, you know, *Noo Yawk*, or *Frasier*, not, basically, student accommodation. It's just full of Chinese business students. You know, you picture yourself sort of borrowing a cup of sugar from the doctor next door, or, I don't know. *No*. It's just – teenagers. You know, whose parents are renting them a flat over here. And there are delivery vans for the Spar starting at five a.m., so it's these reversing-vehicle warning signals blaring out. No chance of a lie-in, or having the windows open in the summer. And, yes, I don't know. I just suddenly realized that everyone else in the building is a student, basically.'

'Nobody told me that,' she said, 'when I was buying the place, which . . . I think they should have done really.'

'They should. That's rotten.'

'Mmm.'

'It's take the money and run, isn't it.'

'Yes. Exactly. Yes. Take the money and run.'

'Well, look. If you like the city but this is making you unhappy then you might have to bite the bullet and move,' I said. 'I know it's easy to say, but you shouldn't hate where you live. Maybe a bit further out?'

'Mmm,' she said. She wasn't sure.

'Maybe somewhere with a garden,' I said.

'Oh yes, I'll get into gardening shall I?' she said, flatly. And then, 'I mean, you picture it being a bit more, you know ... going to the *deli* and buying a "double flat no-fat extra hot frappi-mochaccino to go! Hold the mustard!" kind of thing.'

'I know,' I said. 'But that's like a *Friends* fantasy, isn't it?'

'Mmm,' she said.

'Although, that said, you can't not do that in Manchester. I mean, nowhere's short on coffee shops these days. I suppose we're all living a *Friends* fantasy now, aren't we?' I said.

'Mmm. Maybe.'

'So if it's just the building you're in, maybe now that you've been there a few years you can make a more informed choice?'

'Mmm,' she said.

The waitress was back. Our plates were set down. Here were two large, colourful haystacks of grated vegetables.

'There you go,' I said. 'Nature's bounty.'

'Oh. Gosh,' my mother said.

I got a twinge then.

'Is that OK?' I said. 'We should change it now if it's not,' I said, meanwhile picking up my own knife and fork. I knew she wouldn't want to make a fuss.

'It's fine,' my mother said. 'Yes. Just. Lot of it! Ooh. Yum,' she said.

'OK. Great. Well. Speaking of elaborate meals, how's Michelle doing? How are her culinary ambitions shaping up?'

'What do you mean?' my mother said.

'Didn't you tell me she'd started cooking classes?'

'Oh, yes.'

'And they're going well?'

'I don't know. Yes. I think so. She's always going on about them.'

'And that she was moving house, did you say? Has that all gone through now?'

'Oh, yes. She moved months ago.'

'Have you seen the new place?'

'Oh, yes, just once. I mean I've seen it, but I haven't been in. We drove past and she pointed it out. It was all boxes still, she said.'

'But she's still working in town?'

'Oh, yes. Yes.'

'Does she cook for you?'

'*Well.* No, actually. She'll say, Shall we have lunch on Sunday and I'll say *Yes*, and then they just take me to the pub. So – pub lunches, really.'

'Well, pub lunches are good, too.'

'Mmm.'

'Maybe it's the cooking rather than the cooking *for* somebody she likes. It is nerve-racking to cook for somebody.'

'Yes. Maybe. Mmm.'

My mother was valiant with her detox salad. She took little mouthfuls. Little sips of wine between. Still, my haystack seemed to be shrinking much faster than hers. I tried to give her a chance to catch up. I put my fork down and told her about a film I'd seen which she had said she wanted to see. Although she appeared not to remember having said that now. I told her I'd read a review of one of the exhibitions she was going to see tomorrow. The trouble was, she didn't seem to think she could eat while I was talking. She just held a forkful up ready, and looked nervous. It was only while we were both silent that any real progress was made.

The place was filling up around us. There was a pleasant feeling of bustle and life, and a few interesting-looking characters had arrived; the sort my mother might appreciate, I thought: 'eccentrics'. I just wasn't sure any of it was getting through to her, though. All she was doing, when she wasn't fixing anxiously on my questions, was looking down at her plate.

'How is that?' I said.

'Oh. Well. I *do* like it, yes, but I'm not sure it's going to like *me*, as your grandmother used to say.'

'Oh dear. Really? It's an undertaking, isn't it?'

'Mmm,' she said.

'Come on. Let's down tools,' I said, and I took my glass of wine and sat back in my chair.

'Has veganism taken over Manchester yet?' I said.

She didn't put her knife and fork down, though. And nor did she answer me. Instead she made a show of stopping to wipe her forehead. Then she said, 'Once more unto the breach!'

She stuck her fork into the heap again, bit down on another untidy mouthful and chewed it.

'Mum, let's stop!' I said, with really tremendous good humour and warmth now, and amusement at her little mime. 'There are no prizes for a clean plate. We can have a break.'

'Mum?' I said. 'It's not a challenge.'

But she acted like she hadn't heard me. So less warmly, I said: 'Mum? Mum. Tell me again what you're seeing tomorrow.'

Another forkful. Another frown. She swallowed hard, again. She kept her head down and forked up some more carrot and beetroot; kept going.

Here I stopped saying emollient things.

My mother did clean her plate. She cleaned it and then she put her cutlery down and put her hands on her knees and looked at me – despite everything I'd just said – as if a medal or a badge was exactly what she was going to be given.

'Oh! Well done,' I said, after a moment. 'Gold star for self-punishment.'

'Yes!' she said, smiling.

By then it had been years since I'd taken it into my head to pursue a point with my mother; to chase her down like I used to. But something about the way she was sitting there then, the look on her face . . .

'I've been meaning to ask you this,' I said. 'Do you remember when Dad said he was going to make me a ward of court?'

'Oh. Did he? I don't know.'

'OK, well I do remember. I was about twelve, and I didn't like going on Saturdays so I kept saying I was ill and staying home. He phoned to tell me he'd spoken to his solicitors and he was going to make me a ward of court. He said you were keeping me away from him, and that you'd accused him of – quote – "All sorts of abuse! Sexual things." Unquote. Did you ever say that? It doesn't sound like you. And you weren't keeping me away anyway. I wouldn't go.'

'Oh. I don't know.'

'You'd think you might remember.'

'Well I might have done. I don't know.'

'So you're not saying you didn't? It seems obvious to me that he was lying. He was the liar. I mean, he was the one who'd have an imaginary solicitor. So why not just say he made it up?'

'I don't know.'

'Right.'

The waitress appeared then, and I smiled at her and then kept talking while she took our plates.

'So you didn't say that to anybody. Did you say it when you first left him? Was that why we were in that contact centre?'

My mother made fists with her hands on the table. She was very embarrassed. With the waitress there.

'Mum?' I said.

When the waitress had left, she said, 'I might have done. *I don't know.*'

She was more and more indignant.

'He's dead now – you could deny it, you know. If you did say that.'

No answer.

'Or did you just say it for the sake of it? It's OK. It doesn't matter. It was decades ago. Was it just to score points?'

'*Yes!* Just for the sake of it! Just to score points!'

'Really?'

'I don't remember, *Bridget.* I might have done or I might not have done.'

'Right. OK. I mean, I don't believe you said anything of the sort. It's weird that you won't just admit it.'

My mother sat with her face set. She wasn't going to give me anything.

'No?' I said.

'People do move on, you know,' she said.

'Oh, I think I've moved on,' I said. Mildly. Meanly.

Strange conversation. It really didn't matter, to me. And for her part, my mother was back to her old birthday-girl self with a little coaxing. We paid the bill, climbed the stairs back to the street: it was as if I'd never brought that business up; as if it had never happened.

The following year was the last time we ever met like that; our last birthday meal. On a wet and blowy Tuesday night,

I walked up to Bloomsbury, to a Greek restaurant I'd found, just round the corner from the cinema my mother was coming from. It seemed a safe choice. I knew she liked lamb, and I'd seen her eat a Greek salad. Daphne's looked rather jolly, online, with its ceiling dripping with plastic grapes, and on the back wall, a blown-up photograph of a Cycladean beach. It looked busy and convivial. There even seemed to be some sort of strolling player at large, in a billowy shirt and a gold-buttoned waistcoat, strumming on a guitar which he held vertically. My mother might go for that, I thought, when I booked; for the whole silly scene. I could imagine her saying, 'It's *uncanny*!' As it turned out, it was a good job I hadn't gone into details when I'd told her where to meet, because when I arrived the place was as good as empty. I winced at the idea of her having told the waiter about our reservation.

'I hope this is OK,' I said as I sat down. 'We do have bad luck, don't we? Maybe we should go back to the old groovy Troub.'

'What do you mean?' my mother said.

'Just, you know, last year's beetroot debacle, and now this ghost ship. It's a mistake to try new things. That's the lesson.'

'Why? What's a ghost ship?' she said.

'I mean it's not exactly popular.'

'Oh. I don't know,' she said.

'I suppose it is a cold, rainy Tuesday,' I said, brightly.

After my drink arrived, I found her card in my bag. She smiled and said, 'Coo!' and said she'd save it for tomorrow;

for her *actual* birthday. The lack of present was because I'd made a bold move that Christmas and sent her a whole set of books – the Elena Ferrante books. This was another punt at finding something to talk about. My girlfriends and I had done nothing but talk about them that summer, and I couldn't see why she wouldn't like them. They were full of incident; there were surely situations in there that she would recognize. I also thought my mother might enjoy the 'joining in' aspect of reading them; I knew she'd seen newspaper articles – *Guardian* articles – about the phenomenon; about 'Ferrante fever'. When I was reading them, she'd asked me, 'Have you got "Ferrante fever"?' 'And how!' I'd replied. She would like, I thought, to be part of a phenomenon.

On Boxing Day morning, I got the first text. 'I don't know who anyone is! ☹' she wrote.

'Oh dear,' I said. 'There is a big cast. Don't worry, you soon get used to it.'

A few hours later, my phone peeped again, 'Is Lenu Lina or is Lena Lulu? Argh!'

'Ha ha,' I wrote. 'Maybe write it down?'

So we were talking about the books, in a way. She was joining in, in a way.

Things had gone quiet after that, though, and I had assumed she'd given up, until about a week ago, when she'd started sending the same sort of thing again.

'V confused,' she wrote, 'too many names! Argh!'

'Still waiting for "Ferrante Fever",' she wrote.

'I think you must be immune,' I replied. 'You're a medical miracle.' To which she sent, 'Why medical?'

Now, for want of any other ideas, I said, 'Did you ever get to grips with those books?'

'What do you mean get to grips?' she said.

'The Ferrante books. You were a bit flummoxed by the names.'

'Oh yes. No. I don't know who anybody is.' Here she went straight into the same routine from her text messages. 'Is Lenu Lina or is Lili Lala?' she said. 'No comprendez!'

'How can you follow the plot, then?' I said.

'Oh I can't, no. I haven't got a clue!'

Our food arrived then, so we both leant back and smiled as several little dishes were laid out. Far too many, really: she'd said yes to everything I'd suggested.

'You should probably stop then,' I said. 'Give them to Michelle. She might like them.'

'Oh no,' my mother said. 'I've started so I'll finish,' she said in her Magnus Magnusson voice.

'How far in are you? Are you still on book one?'

'Oh no, halfway through book *two* now.'

'But how can you read it if you haven't got the two lead characters straight?'

'Well. I don't *know*.'

Trying to move the conversation on, I said,

'The end of book one is where I got really hooked, I think. That's when it kicked in.'

She showed her teeth here.

'Oh yes. What's that?'

'The wedding.'

'Oh yes. Whose wedding?'

She said this still grinning at me. As if I were meant to find all of this charming. In truth I felt very much not up for it. But this was my own doing, so I went for warm exasperation.

'Oh for Christ's sake, Mum! It was a bad present. Give them to Oxfam, or to Michelle.'

'Oh no. I've started so I'll finish,' she said, again, making her voice sound deep and Icelandic.

'OK. Well, look. I thought they might give us something to talk about,' I said, 'You know, now *Mad Men*'s finished. But if you're reading it without reading it, then that's not the idea. I don't want any more texts about how lost you are, please. *That* I'm not interested in. Read it or don't, but no more of this who's who, please.'

'Ooh,' she said, 'OK. No more texts. Mustn't ... text ... Bridget,' she said, as if she were writing it down.

I tipped some salad onto my plate. I reached for a strip of pitta bread: the last one, so I tore it in two. My mother took a stuffed vine leaf and set to trying to cut it up with what was evidently a rather blunt knife.

'Well,' I said. 'Anyway. How's your flat? Are you selling up or toughing it out?'

'Oh,' she said, 'it's the same. Yes. Same, really.'

'But you're staying on?'

'Oh, I don't know, Bridge,' she said. 'You don't just snap your fingers and move you know.'

'I know. Sorry.'

'What about Griff?' I said. 'How's he?'

'I don't know,' she said. 'Ask him.'

'Mum, you can text me about the books,' I said, 'I was just being grumpy.'

'Mmm,' she said. 'Well. OK.'

More little plates were set down. Some more wine was poured. My mother fixed on the waiter as he filled her glass. Her hands were in loose little fists on the table.

'So how's Manchester's buzzing arts scene?' I said.

'Oh. Well . . .' she said.

'Any new talent to report?' I said, brightly.

'Well, yes,' she said, 'funny you should ask. There has been a little bit of drama, although, well, I don't know.'

'Go on.'

'Well, bit of back story . . . For years, when I've been out at various events I've seen this very nice man who seems to know everybody but who *did* seem to be single and not gay. Now I knew his name was Malc because I had overheard people say Oh, hi Malc. He always wears a blue spotted neck scarf and he looks a bit like, well, a gypsy, I suppose you'd say.'

'*So* – cut to – just before Christmas. I was going to this Festive Fun drinks do at the Castlefield Gallery. Only at the last minute Michelle said she'd come with me, because we were on the phone and she said what are you up to. *So.* Off we go. Only we'd no sooner got our drinks and started, you know, mingling, than Malc, who, as I say, had never noticed

I *existed* before, was suddenly sort of hailing us. Waving at us as if we were his long-lost relatives! Well, as it turned out, it was Michelle he was hailing, because that pub she worked in when she was a student was his local, down in Salford. So he remembered her from there.'

'That was good luck,' I said. 'You had an in.'

'I had an in, yes! And, yes, we just spent the whole night chatting, then. Just, you know, like a house on fire.'

'Am I sensing there's a but on the horizon?'

'Well you are, yes, there was. So – a few weeks later, *picture the scene*,' she said, 'I was at this talk at the Whitworth, and I had thought he might be there, because I've seen him there before, and I walk in and there he was, so I sort of went over and stood near where he was standing, and then, you know, acted casual, but – no reaction, so finally I just said "Oh, hello," and – nothing. Just a total blank face. So I said, "I'm Michelle's mum." "Oh!" he said. "That's right! Michelle's Mum" and he asked if Michelle was with me, and I said No, and then there was just total silence. No, you know, How have you been? Or, What have you been up to? Nothing.'

'Oh dear,' I said.

'Yes,' she said, 'and then I sort of stayed standing in his area after the talk, you know, by the coffee urn, and a couple of other people came over then, friends of his I suppose, and because I was standing there, they looked at me like "who's this?" and so he said, "And this is *Michelle's Mum*."'

'That's a bit rude.'

'Yes. And I said, "It's *Hen*," but no one listened. This couple just said, "Hello, Michelle's Mum!"'

'Maybe if it happens again,' I said, 'say, "I'm Helen Grant, we met at the Castlefield Gallery with my daughter, Michelle."'

'Mmm. Well. So, you know, I did stay sort of standing in his group, and the *crowd thinned out* and no one has asked me anything or spoken to me, or even acknowledged my existence really, they were all just discussing something *they* were doing at the weekend, so finally I just said, "Well, I'm going now. Time to hit the road!" and he said, "Goodbye Michelle's Mum." And then just went back to his conversation.'

'Oh dear. Well, I'm glad you did leave. Doesn't sound like he was overburdened with manners.'

'No,' she said. 'Well, the next week I went along, same place, for the next talk in the series, and it was exactly the same. I spotted him, went over, said, "Hello Malc!" *Nothing*. Totally blank look. So I said, "I'm *Michelle's* mum." And it was the same again, he says, "Oh. Hello, Michelle's Mum."'

'Why did you do that?' I said.

'Do what?'

'Well, *a*, go over, and *b*, say "I'm Michelle's mum".'

She frowned, then carried on with her story, which was the same story she'd just told me. Same words. Same outcome.

'And when I said, *Well*, I'd better be going now, he said, "Goodbye Michelle's Mum." Exactly the same. *Exactly*. So.'

'Right,' I said.

It was the usual formula. The theme was exclusion. The mood was wounded shock. But she spoke so eagerly. As when she was telling me about bad films, or broken slide projectors.

'I do not understand your life,' I said now.

And she said, 'No! *Well.*'

She was even more cheerful later on that night when she told me how a woman in her aquarobics class had died.

'Oh, it was terrible,' she said. 'I thought she was going a bit funny, but then a lot of the people there are quite "eccentric" so you just sort of let it go. She used to be very loud and bossy, but the last few weeks I did notice that she'd gone quiet. After class she started to just sit on the bench in the changing room. Everyone else would be dressed and she'd be sitting there still in her cossie. Just completely still, completely silent. I said once, Are you OK Amanda? But she didn't answer. Anyway, obviously something went pop, because apparently she just didn't wake up. Her husband woke up with, you know, a dead body. So that was all the talk in the changing room last week and the instructor said a little speech about her "untimely" death. Because she was one of the younger members. She was younger than me. So, *yes.*'

'You never know the foggy Friday,' I said.

This was one of her phrases, brought out in my childhood whenever anyone died, an acquaintance or a celebrity. It was somewhere between a warning and a gotcha. I don't know where she'd picked it up.

'Yes!' she said now, pleased. '*You never know the foggy Friday.* So.'

'Shall we have a brandy with our coffees?' I said.

While I was trying to raise the waiter for our bill, my mother asked me about my new flat. She knew I'd just bought a place with John. Both the boyfriend and the move had the potential to upset her, so I had tried to play the whole thing down. I'd told her that the street was a bit dingy, and noisy at night; that it was a long uphill walk from the Tube. And now, faced with her brave look, I went helplessly off on the same tack again. I went further. I made it sound like we were living in a cold-water room in a crime zone. For her part, she kept very still while I spoke – her hands, again, gripping the edge of the table. I quickly realized it didn't really matter what I said. I'd got myself in a spot again. And as when we used to talk about her crushes, I felt that what I said was being scrabbled through for some currency quite other than meaning or information: rather for the glitter of that old magic coin, the token she could hold tightly and exchange for entry, for a real welcome, into her imagined other place.

I didn't know how to fend that off. Or maybe I was too tired to try. I just kept talking. It was great that John could work from home now, I said. And it was nice to have a little patch of garden for the cat. I reached for my phone to get a photo of him.

'And have you got a spare room?' my mother said.

'Oh. No.'

'Well a sofa, then?'

'No. Why?'

'You don't have a sofa? Where do you sit, hey?'

'No. I mean, why are you asking about a spare room and a sofa?'

'Oh. I just thought ... be nice to stay, maybe, next year, instead of a hotel.'

'On our sofa?' I said.

'Well,' she said. 'I don't know. I could.'

'That doesn't make sense,' I said. 'You can afford a hotel.'

'Our sofa is pretty lumpy, actually,' I said, with a smile. Another lie. And another misstep. I could feel, I could tell, she was going to pounce now, going to gamely say, 'I don't mind lumpy!' Well, I killed that impulse. I dropped my smile, checked my watch.

'Are we going Dutch?' I said.

She frowned and reached for her bag. She sat there holding her card.

'Bridge?' she said. 'Bridge? Why aren't I allowed to meet John?'

'Allowed?' I said, but the waiter arrived then with his card reader, and while we tapped in our PINs, she looked pained, because he was there, and so she couldn't say anything. I didn't mind who heard us, however. I never minded a witness.

'Why do you say "allowed"?' I said.

She was still looking at the waiter. Her eyes were fixed on him. 'Where do you get these words?' I said. I tried to say it in a friendly way, a letting-out-the-tension way.

She didn't answer me. She looked sullen. Scolded. Not put off, however, and once we'd stood and put our coats and hats and scarves back on, once I'd pushed open the heavy glass door and we were back out in the cold night and alone again, I heard how being welcomed into your daughter's home was *normal*, and meeting your daughter's boyfriend was *normal*.

'Is it?' I said. And, 'Right.'

'We're normal now, are we?' I said, still trying to keep the mood light, as I checked on my phone that I was walking the right way.

'*Everyone* meets their children's boyfriends,' she was saying now, urgently, insistently, her little steps trying to keep up with my longer stride. I was walking with the tight-lipped and blinkered intent of someone leaving a crime scene.

'It's so *embarrassing*,' my mother said, 'when people *ask*.'

'Well, well,' I said, and then, '*Fuck*. Wrong way.'

I turned about, looked for Malet Street. She continued to press her case as we walked back the way we'd come. She made her one point repeatedly. Made it with the toneless insistence of a locked-out cat. People *asked*. She didn't know what to *tell them*. As with my father's pub fantasy, I wanted to say, What bloody people? But that would have been cruel, wouldn't it? So she had me there.

It did strike me, though, that at least those spectral associates my father raised didn't persecute him. They were a supporting cast: a wise counsel or a happy coterie, rushing in to fill coveted positions in his court. Leave it to my poor mother to have these awful tormenting busybodies as her imaginary fellows.

By the Tube barriers, I said, 'Well. Happy birthday, Mum,' and she stood very still then, like a column, while I held her narrow shoulders and touched my cheek to her cheek.

It was nearly midnight when I got home. John was away, and I was late, and Puss appeared from the bedroom complaining about that, so I picked him up and carried him through to the kitchen, where I helped him to clamber from my shoulder to the top of the boiler cupboard. Only it turned out that wasn't where he wanted to be either, and he started to find his way back down. He was an old cat. These were drops which he took cautiously, judiciously: to the back of the armchair, then the chair seat, then the floor.

His china bowl said CAT. I picked that up, then stepped around him and found his Whiskas. The jelly-envelope of fish chunks slid into the bowl, and I used his special fork to mash the mixture up.

I loved being in our flat. I loved closing the door behind me. And seeing to the cat, and tidying up – making the place nice. I was unloading the dishwasher when I heard my phone ringing, in my coat pocket, out in the hall. It was my mother calling.

'Bridge?' she said.

'Hello? Yes, it's me.'

'Now Bridge, after all that I forgot to give you your present!'

'Oh God, never mind!'

'Well—'

'Save it for next year. Or drop it in the post. You've got the new address.'

'Yes, I'm outside.'

'Outside where?'

'I've brought your present. I'm outside *22B* . . .'

'You're here?'

'Yes, I'm outside. I pressed the bell.'

I went round the corner, still holding my phone to my ear. There was a shape at the little diamond window in the door. A mother-shaped shape.

'Hello Bridge!' she said. 'I was just about to step on the train when I thought, hmm . . . this bag's a bit heavy!'

She handed me the parcel.

'Thank you,' I said. 'There was no need to come for that.'

'Oh. Well. May as well. Save a stamp. I did press the bell,' she said, again, as if it were the phone call that was the intrusion.

'Right. Yeah. That doesn't always work.'

She shivered in her coat. Grinned. This was exciting. Different. Had she brought this off?

I wasn't lying about the dingy street, or the distance from the station. She had been intrepid.

'So can I have the grand tour?' she said.

'Oh. Well.'

'Are you not going to ask me in?'

'Sure. It is quite late, though.'

'Can I just use your loo, then?' she said. 'I'm desperate.'

'No you're not.'

'I am. I *am*.'

'I don't believe you,' I said, standing aside.

'I'll just go here then shall I?' she said. 'I'll just do it here.'

'I'm letting you in,' I said. 'Come on!'

I stood in the kitchen and heard the toilet flush and then the tap running.

'Nice bathroom!' my mother said when she came in.

'Oh, thanks.'

'No John?' she said, making to peep round the corner to where the living room was.

'Not tonight, no.'

'Is he away?'

'He is.'

'Can I have a quick look round, Bridge?'

'I can't stop you. I mean, it will be quick, because there isn't that much of it. This is the living room-stroke-kitchen-stroke-dining room. We sleep through there. You can see the garden through there. It's small but there's room for a table, so in the summer that should be nice.'

I stepped over to the kitchen window, expecting her to follow and look out. She was more interested in what was behind her though, back in the hallway.

'That looks like a spare room,' she said.

'That is John's study. And his consulting room now. You can't go in there. *I* can't go in there.'

'Coo!' she said.

'His clients go in through the garden. I work in there,' I

said, nodding at the door behind her, but she was heading back to the kitchen now. I followed her in and found her leaning over the sink to peer through the window at the garden.

She wasn't there for long, just fifteen minutes or so. She said yes to a coffee but didn't touch the one I made. When I yawned, she said she'd best be going, and I walked her to the door, where she stepped out very cheerfully, into the drizzle. At the gate, she stopped and looked around. She put a finger to her lips and turned to the right and then to the left.

'Do you want a taxi?' I called out, and she considered that and then agreed.

Back in the living room, we watched the car approaching on my phone screen, the little icon moving as if on castors, like a planchette . . .

When it started nosing blindly at the corner of our street, my mother broke away and rushed to the door.

'We're going to miss it!' she said.

'Come on!' she said. 'Let me out, Bridge!'

'He's going to go without me!' she said.

IV

1

The Clan Grant Society holds its annual Gathering every August, in Grantown-on-Spey in the Cairngorms. Hundreds of Grants attend, coming from all over the world for a long weekend of activities and events. The highlight is the Clan March, on the Saturday morning, when the assembled Grants process together behind flag bearers and massed pipe bands and drums, to the Abernethy Highland Games.

My mother was a Grant by marriage – and my father had made nothing of his Scottish descent – but after she moved to Manchester she joined the society and every year took the long train journey north for the Gathering.

One year, as a Christmas present to herself, she bought a Clan Grant brooch, embossed with their motto 'Stand Fast', and with the silver fashioned into the clan crest: a fire burning on Craig Elachie. This was a signal fire, used to rally the clan before an attack. She explained all of this to me, having worn the brooch one year to our meeting in the Troubadour. Craig Elachie meant Rock of Alarm, she said, rolling her rs and hocking up the *ch*. With clenched fists and her head held high, with wild, Private Frazer eyes, she declaimed her creed:

'Stand Fast, Craig Elachie!'

In the summer after that fearsome raid on my flat, my mother went, as usual, up to Grantown, where the activity of the weekend that year was a Monarch of the Glen walking tour. She was clambering over the moorland with her fellows, a long way from the coach, when she caught her foot in a rabbit hole and, as she put it later, her knee 'just went'.

Even supported by two sturdy Grants it was too far for her to hobble back to the car park, so she was deposited back on the spongy ground, where, she said, she watched her knee swell up 'like a balloon'. Somebody called Highland Rescue, and they sent an air ambulance.

My mother texted me an account of all this later that night, from her bed in Raigmore Hospital: 'Knee gone. Airlifted to Inverness.' I boggled imagining the scene. My mother lashed to a stretcher, winched into the air. My mother dangling against the blue Scottish sky. Plaything of the wind. And all of those gathered Grants below, scattered on the hillside, gazing up at this extraordinary departure.

I'd got that wrong, I discovered, when I called her. The helicopter could land. But still. My mother in a *helicopter*. Had she been frightened?

'Oh no,' she said, indignantly.

Excited?

'No. Why excited?' she said.

And I remembered then that image I'd had of her when she was out with Griff: borne through life. And now through the empyrean. Of course it was fitting. Of course she found my question strange. Why would she be excited?

She did seem pleased – or rather, satisfied – to have an email from the Clan chief, wishing her a 'speedy recovery'.

At Christmas that year, in place of her birthday plans, I got an email with the subject line: 'KNEE UPDATE'.

'Got date for knee op. It would be a great help, as I shall be on 2 crutches and unable to go out for 7 weeks, if you could come and stay for 1 week in Feb days tbc. Blanket baths and bum wiping not required! Mum'

On the day, I texted, 'Good luck' and the next afternoon, 'How did it go?'

'Griff is doing a great job looking after me. It would be great if you could come up sometime in Feb.'

'When are you coming?' she wrote the next day.

The emails came frequently, too, for those first three weeks, headed 'PROGRESS REPORT' and 'KNEE LATEST' and, twice, 'YOUR VISIT'. 'Don't worry,' she repeated, 'no bed baths or bum-wiping required!' Hard, then, to see what was required, I thought. She could have her shopping delivered, couldn't she? I texted to say I couldn't stay for a whole week because I had to work, but I might manage a few days.

'Good,' she replied. Things went quiet after that. At the end of January I wrote asking how she was feeling, and would next weekend be any use?

'Next week fine,' she wrote. 'I am OK thanks although I've had a few setbacks.'

'Oh dear. What happened?'

I didn't think she'd answer that, but her reply came by return.

'Setbacks were horrendous panic attacks with me in the corridor shouting I can't breathe and trying to rip my clothes off and my leg swelled up so I was in A&E for 6 hours last Saturday until they decided it wasn't DVT. The physio is hard but quite fun in the pool with others.'

'Oh dear!' I wrote, again. 'Great that you are back in the water, though.'

My mother's building was behind Oxford Road station. Her phone was engaged when I arrived, but I had the access codes for the outer gate and then the lobby. Inside, it really did look like a hall of residence; it reminded me of my own, with bike wheel scuffs on the floor tiles, and a spread of night club flyers on top of the mailboxes. In the lift, there were shiny pizza menus on the floor, and a sticker on the mirror advertising a rape hotline.

My mother was waiting in the open door of her flat, leaning on her crutches.

'Sorry! Sorry Bridge. The phone rang and it was Griff and he just wouldn't let me go!'

She looked very small, slung between those two grey struts. She looked older, too, but then it must have been years since I'd seen her in daylight – albeit the daylight that the corridor admitted was rather muted. She was wearing her green polo neck and some black linen trousers with a drawstring waist. On her feet she had white bobbled sports socks and her moccasin slippers. Slowly she swung herself back down the hallway.

When she bought this flat, she described it to me as 'loft style', 'open plan'. She'd been happy that it came fully furnished, too, because she had nothing. In her living room-stroke-kitchen, there was a grey leather sofa and a matching swivel armchair. There was a smoked-glass coffee table and a little round dining table that matched that. I recognized them from the brochure she'd forwarded. Now there was also a black wood shelving unit, which held some books and DVDs, and some ornaments from my grandmother's flat. The maracas were there. The bookends. But the room looked rather bare, overall. You wouldn't have guessed she'd been there as long as she had. There were plastic storage crates stacked against the back wall, apparently not unpacked since the move. There were cardboard boxes, labelled MISC., on top of the kitchen cupboards. The chief sign of current occupancy was the piles of old *Guardians* everywhere: just like when I was small, when the *Guardian Guides* which she 'hadn't read yet!' would number in the dozens.

Now she lowered herself onto the settee and moved the cushions about.

'Do you need anything? I said. 'Shall I put the kettle on?'

'Well, I did just boil it, so ... if you could make a cup of tea, yes that would be nice. Thank you. And if you go out the way we came in, your room, the *guest room*, is the door on the left.'

With the tea made, I sat in the swivel armchair and wheeled it up closer. The television was on but *Coronation Street* had been paused. The scene was set in the Kabin. Like us, Rita and Norris were both holding tea mugs.

'You can set that going if you want,' I said.

'OK, yes please. I do need to catch up.'

She picked up the remote and pointed it at the set.

Behind the TV, a picture window showed a dull white sky and the corner of a multi-storey car park. On the window itself, in the middle of the flat's windscreen, so to speak, there was a print – I don't know what else to call it – of a pigeon: a pigeon's neck and head, and a pigeon's spread wings. I stood up to get a closer look at that. The details of the feathers could be seen. Individual barbs.

'How did this happen?' I said.

My mother winced; she paused her programme again and squinted at me.

'This thing,' I said.

'Oh, yes. Well, I don't know. I just heard a bang one day last week and hopped in here and yes, there it was. I don't know how to clean it off.'

'Do you think the pigeon made it?'

'What do you mean?'

'Sorry. I mean, do you think the pigeon survived?'

'Well, I don't know.'

'It's a bit like the Turin shroud.'

'How's that?'

'Oh, you know. An eerie impression. You know what the Turin shroud is.'

'Do I? Well. I don't know.'

I sat back down. That was going nowhere.

'Let's see then,' I said, nodding at my mother's outstretched leg.

'Oh, do you want to see it? Well, not for the squeamish! Here we go.'

She pulled up her trouser leg to show the knee, which was thickly bandaged. It was melon-sized.

'Bloody hell,' I said.

'I know,' she said. 'And. Just a sec.'

She undid the safety pin and rolled the bandage back, carefully, until I could see the end of the scar: spiky black stitches, and the skin around them shiny, hot pink, and creased in close darts.

'Ouch.'

'Yes, it is ouch! Terribly painful. And at night . . . You can't get comfy.'

'Oh dear. Are you on lots of painkillers?'

'Yes. Yes I am. But I can't sleep, *at all*. And – yes, it's not much fun being trapped in here. Although, Griff's been good. He helps me bring the shopping in, because you can order it, but if you aren't there instantly they drive away. So when I make an order he comes and sort of lies in wait. And he's also taken it upon himself to tell my various groups why I'm not there, so I've got all these cards, *which is nice*. And he took me out last weekend, out to Alderley Edge, so . . .'

'That's good. So you have been out.'

'I've been out several times.'

'Oh. OK. And what did you do in Alderley Edge?'

'Well, we had a *pub lunch*, yes, that was nice. But, good God, Griff! Nothing is ever right.'

'No? He's still his old self is he?'

'He's getting worse and worse. He made this big show of telling the waiter he was gluten intolerant, which – first I've heard of it. So they were all fussing around and checking labels, oh you can have this or this and our chef can make *this*, only then, having eaten this huge chicken casserole with roast potatoes *and* chips on the side – I mean, roast potatoes *and* chips – of course he wants pudding, too. "Oh we're terribly sorry, sir, none of the desserts are guaranteed gluten free but what we can do is make you a fruit salad." Well, you can imagine, *fruit salad*. No. So then he just orders chocolate cake. Oh that's not gluten free, sir, unfortunately. Well, he just said it would be fine. Having made such a fuss. Having had this special gravy made. And all these people scurrying around him. I mean . . .'

'He makes his presence felt, doesn't he?'

'Well. Yes. Yes he does.'

'What's happening in *Coronation Street* these days? Is it good?'

'Oh. Yes. I mean, I can't explain it all now.'

'I wasn't asking you to explain it. I was just showing an interest. I do have a question, though. Why are you catching up if you've been stuck in here for weeks?'

'Well. Hmm. That is a good question! I don't know. I just always save them up.'

'You can put it on again. Sorry. No more interruptions.'

She reached for her remote. I went and got my book from my bag. She had the television on very loud, though, and after an hour or so of that, I was feeling quite trapped myself.

'What have you got in for tonight, Mum?' I said.

She frowned again, pressed pause.

'What's that?'

'Just wondering what you've got in for tonight. Do you want me to go to the shop, or do you want to get a takeaway? Is there anything you fancy?'

'Ooh,' she said, 'I don't know. I did get a shop yesterday, so . . .'

'OK, I'll have a look.'

There were a lot of ready meals in the fridge. Nothing without meat or cheese.

'Is there anything to drink hidden around here?' I said.

'Oh. Yes. There's a box out in the hall. That's my wine cellar. Or at the back of the fridge there should be a can of gin and tonic. That's Griff's really, but I'm sure you could have it.'

'I can't see anything I could eat. I might go out and buy some vegetables. Shall I make us a vegetable curry? I can do a nice one.'

'Ooh. OK.'

'I'll take the keys. You don't have to get up. Have you got any tote bags?'

'Have I got any tote bags? I've got the world's biggest collection of tote bags! I can't go anywhere without being given a tote bag! I'm *drowning* in . . .'

'Where are they?' I said.

My mother was right. Her building and the streets around it were lousy with students. In Sainsbury's the only people her age were serving at the tills, as far as I could see. So . . . what did I need? A cauliflower, first, then a tin of chickpeas and a tin of tomatoes; a box of ground cumin – she wouldn't have that, would she? – then back to the vegetable aisle for garlic and ginger and fresh coriander, then back to the spices for some ground coriander. Next a plastic drum of poppadoms and a jar of mango chutney. A pot of soy yogurt. Back to the vegetables for a cucumber. What a stupid idea this had been! And as for asking her if she needed anything. She'd told me herself she'd just had a delivery. Still, there I was with her list, which would need another basket.

On the way back, I stopped at the Caffè Nero by the station. In there, too, there were only a couple of people in my mother's age group: one man who looked like a down-and-out, and another who was sitting with his talkative student son. My mother was sixty-eight and living in a student block in a student area, behind sooty railway arches, with throbbing music from the club over the way, which, she told me, didn't stop until two a.m. at the weekend. With chip trays left in the corridor. With refrigerator lighting. How had she not noticed when she'd viewed the place? Should I have gone up to see her when she'd first moved? In another world Michelle and I would both have gone with her to the viewings, and we all would have sat together afterwards, looking through the brochures, imagining her new life ... as energized by possibility as those groups of happy women in the Nero photographs.

Back in the flat, *Coronation Street* was still going on.

'Do you need it that loud, Mum? I could hear it out in the corridor.'

Again, my mother winced at the interruption. She reached for the remote to point and pause.

'What's that?'

'Just asking if it has to be so loud. You can hear it outside.'

'Can you. Oh. Well I'm completely deaf so yes it does yes.'

'Are you? Oh. OK.'

I opened the freezer to put away the ready meals she'd asked for, and as expected, found the drawers there already packed with the same type: stacks of salmon tagliatelle; stacks of lasagne. When I pointed this out she said,

'You asked if you could get me anything.'

And yes, I suppose I had.

'OK,' I said, 'I'll shut up now. Promise.'

She squeezed the button again, set the larky Weatherfield figures going again, loudly, while I set out what I'd need to cook tea.

Was she deaf? She had always liked a loud TV. When I was small, she ate her tea from a tray on her lap in 'her' living room watching a loud TV, and it was the same routine then, with the persecuted look if I went in to ask her something. Even if I just stood in the doorway, seeing what was on. She said I was 'looming over' her. 'Stop looming over me, you're like the sword of Damocles,' she'd say. And when I left, as I went back into the kitchen or upstairs, I would hear her turn the volume up further. Just a touch. Just for a moment. To resettle herself, I suppose.

I chopped and fried, and stirred and simmered. I sliced open the poppadom packet. I said, 'OK! We leave that for forty-five minutes now,' and got no reply, so went back to the spare room and sat on the bed, though the thin walls could not keep out that bloody mournful trumpet theme.

There were storage crates in that room, too. I opened one – there were some *Computing* magazines, from the nineties, and a tangle of old black tights. Next I looked in the drawers in the bedside cabinet. They were all empty. I looked under the bed: nothing. The small window gave onto the car park . . .

I recognized the clock-radio; the white plastic clock-radio-cassette player. That used to live in the kitchen in the old house, and was the source of the music my mother would do her dances to. It was what she used to play her Phil Spector Christmas tape on, throughout December, every year, *ring-ting-tingaling* me to the very end of my last nerve. The battery door was held down now by a jagged piece of brown parcel tape, but either the battery was dead or the whole thing was broken. I couldn't make it work.

As I laid the table my mother pressed pause and hoisted herself up, with a 'One-two-three-and!'

'How are you feeling?' I said.

'Coo!' she said, at the knives and forks and wine glasses.

It was strange to sit down like that in her flat, at the tiny glass table, at the two café chairs: it felt like we were doing a bit of studio theatre. I poured out two glasses of red wine and served her some curry and showed her the spoons for the chutney and the yogurt.

'Do you make this for *John*?' my mother said.

'Mmm,' I said.

And then, 'Yes, sometimes. It's quite quick. But he does most of the cooking, you know.'

'And is John a *vegan*?'

'Well. I want to say not yet. But after however many years, I don't think he's going to come over now! He's a vegetarian. So, he cooks for both of us, and then he puts cheese on top of his.'

Next to my chair, keeping me somewhat hemmed in, were another couple of clear plastic storage baskets. These looked to be filled with papers and cardboard folders.

'What's all this?' I said.

'Oh. All that is photographs and letters and postcards and old ration cards and old cinema tickets and all sorts. Just all sorts. There was just this huge box of *stuff* in your grandma's house that I'd never looked through so I thought I'd sort that all out. So I'm doing the photographs first, just sorting them into different places or people. Although, I don't know who half of them are! So I'm just putting them in different folders for now.'

'And then what? Will they go in albums?'

'Hm ... No, I don't think so.'

'OK.'

'Are they his photos? Grandpa's, I mean.'

'Well some of them are. There are lots he took at Tangmere. And then Maracaibo. Then the older ones are his family, but obviously he didn't take them. Those are Edwardians, practically, some of them! And just various ... well, I don't know who they are!'

'Do you still have his Polaroid camera?'

'Do I? Hmm ... No. Don't think so. I think Joe had that off me.'

'Right ... Can I see?'

'Well. Not ... Can you wait till I've sorted them? I mean ... I'll forget where everything goes!'

'OK!' I said. And then, 'How's that?' I said, about the food.

'Oh yes, fine, yes,' my mother said. 'Yum. Yes.'

'Is there anything on to watch after dinner?' I said. 'Anything I can understand from scratch?'

'Oh. Yes, well, Saturday night is Scandi night on BBC Four, so we could put that on.'

'Ah, great, OK.'

I poured another glass of wine for myself. I asked about Griff and Michelle. I asked, forgetting that I'd already asked, whether she'd had any nice cards.

'Oh yes, lots,' she said, 'I mean, they're all there. You've seen them. I've had all sorts of cards.'

At seven a.m., I was back in Nero, having a bag of raisins and a coffee, reading the *Sunday Times*. When I got back my mother wasn't up, but I could hear the radio on in her bedroom. *Sounds of the Sixties*. I knocked and asked if she wanted anything. She thought for a moment but then said she was OK, thanks, for now. Then she called me back to say I could take her tea mug back to the kitchen for her. I did that, and then I unloaded the dishwasher. With nothing else to do, I went back to lie on the bed in the spare room, reading my book.

Once my mother was up I went out and sat with her for a while. She asked me to get her *Observer* from the mailbox downstairs, so I did. Then she sat, or rather lay down, on the settee, doing the sudoku.

I tried to make conversation about the headlines, but was only met with a lot of 'Mmms' and some facetious nodding, so again I went back to the spare room, back to my book, which again I read with terrible concentration, feeling guilty and angry, and restless from lack of exercise, and mucky from lack of a bath.

Just when I was calming down, my mother started humming. I'd forgotten about that habit. She was out in the hallway humming the 'Queen of the Night' aria from *The Magic Flute*.

'Do you have to hum?' I said, sticking my head out of the door.

'What do you mean?'

'It's very loud and repetitive. Could you stop? I'm trying to read.'

But even as I said that I was sitting back down on the bed and lacing up one boot, and then reaching for the other one, so I could go out for my second walk of the morning.

'Oh!' my mother was saying. 'Pardon me for humming a happy tune.'

'Does John never sing a happy tune?' she said, as I headed towards the front door with my coat half on.

'Do you tell John off for singing a happy tune?' my mother said.

'I'm just nipping out for a bit of air,' I said. 'Text me if you think of anything you need!'

Outside, the 'air' was dingy with fumes. Oxford Road was a wall of buses. I walked up towards Piccadilly and sat in a different Nero.

One brainwave I'd had was to help my mother to do something about her hoarding: the Stack 'n' Store baskets that narrowed the hallway and squatted in the corners of each room. She shouldn't be able to say no to that. It was attention; being fussed over. She could be teased about her incorrigibility. It would cheer me up, too. I'd grown up surrounded by shit, and I always enjoyed getting rid of it. This would pass the time and we could both feel good.

When I got back in, I said, 'Shall we do some sorting, Mum? Go through some of these boxes. They're in your way on those crutches, aren't they?'

'Oh!' she said. 'OK, yes.'

'Let's start with all your accessories.'

She sat on the settee and I brought in the crates. I gave her a bin bag, and I designated a spot for the charity pile, for the keep pile and for the recycling pile. Then I held up each item in turn. My approach was briskly sceptical. We quickly established that though she could try to make a case for items I'd condemned, I wasn't going to have it, and that was all part of the fun! I was just like one of those daytime TV presenters!

Here, for example, were four tatty black handbags.

'Now they are all slightly different, you see,' my mother ventured.

'They're bust, Mum. This one's got a broken zip. This one's lining's torn. And you don't need four of anything.'

'Well, as your Nana Barnes used to say, they don't *eat* anything, do they?'

'They eat space. And they eat time when you're trying to get ready. You've got this nice one.'

'Well, that one's for best.'

'Oh, come on. What is it you say? "You never know the foggy Friday." Just use the nice one.'

Was she won over? Even slightly titillated by my invoking her death? She was.

'OK. *Yes.*'

She was remarkably amenable. We did her scarf box next and then her winter hat crate, and then that crate of magazines and tangled tights.

'Now let's rationalize your tote bags,' I said.

'OK!'

'We can keep the ones that are a useful size, *and* we can keep the conversation starters.'

'Oh yes!' she said.

Finally – she suggested this, I was getting tired – we went through her bathroom things: two plastic crates of medicine, toiletries and make-up. I brought them into the living room, stacked them by the settee.

'What have you been carting all this around for?' I said, and she grinned at that.

First out of the first box were several empty, sticky cough medicine bottles. Then a broken LadyShave. There was a metal tube of Bonjela, curled up like a snail and coated in talcum powder.

I passed my mother a bottle of baby Calpol with a rusted lid, and then a baby thermometer and a box of dried-out old Mr. Men plasters.

'Bin?' I said.

'*Yes,*' she said, and she dropped them into the black bag.

Here was another familiar item: a bottle of Mackenzies smelling salts. In fact, looking through the soft debris of cotton balls and flattened plaster boxes, I found half a dozen of those palm-sized brown bottles, which my mother used to keep everywhere: by her bed, in her coat pockets, in the glove compartment of her car. 'I'm not sure there's much charge left in that,' I said, sniffing one, then passing it over. She was reluctant to get rid of them all, though. To see which was worth keeping, she started sniffing each one in turn. Meanwhile, I had a sniff of a yellowish tincture I used to paint on the warts around my fingernails when I was small. That took me back.

Here was half a roll of Extra Strong Mints which had congealed into one sticky cylinder.

And here were several huge sanitary pads with pale dust in the creases.

I stacked up three partially used tubs of Andrews Liver Salts.

'We can rationalize these,' I said.

In the make-up crate there were nine bottles and three tubes of old foundation. I lined them up on the coffee table, and then dabbed the contents of one on the back of my hand. It was thick and apricot coloured, and it quickly 'set'.

'This is like stage make-up,' I said. 'Or industrial paint. Was it this colour originally?'

'Oh yes,' my mother said. 'That was the style!'

'Were you this colour?' I said.

'Oh. I don't know!' she said. 'Maybe!'

We sorted through dried-out mascaras and a clatter of glued-shut nail polish bottles.

That purple lipstick might come back in was arguable, but I persuaded my mother that it would not come back in for *her* ...

Energized by that tussle, which was a close run thing, she won the next point, against a worn-out opponent, over a pale blue Mary Quant eyeshadow.

'Now that is a *collector's item*,' my mother said, firmly, putting it in her small 'keep' pile.

'There are a lot of scrunched-up tissues here,' I said. 'I think they can go, can't they?'

Grey skies. Raindrops chasing down the window. That pigeon print was still there, though. Pigeon in displayed attitude: an emblem of our plight. There was the sound of the wind bashing a loose bit of plastic sheeting on the scaffolding opposite.

'I feel like we're out at sea,' I said as we sat down for lunch: a bowl of soup and a few oatcakes.

'What do you mean?' my mother said.

'But I suppose it's not so bad to be housebound when it's miserable out.'

'Mmm,' she said.

'Are you missing society?'

'Oh. Maybe. I don't know.'

'You're not going stir crazy? I am, and it's only been twenty-four hours.'

'I do feel I'm going a *bit* mad,' she said. 'But I feel that anyway, really. Even when I'm out every night. There's nowhere to walk here. I used to love long walks. Here you always feel trapped.'

'In Manchester?'

'Mmm. You'd have to get on a train, really. There's no parks in town. Nowhere to go. I mean, if you want a long walk there's nothing.'

'Did you walk in Liverpool?'

'A little bit, yes. We went to Sefton Park. But I mean London, really. The river. I used to love walking there.'

'Gosh. Did you?'

'Mmm.'

'There's the water park here, isn't there?' I said, never having been there, and I didn't suppose it was much like the Thames. 'But that's a bus ride, I suppose.'

'Mmm,' my mother said, again.

'Do you and John get out much? Walks and things?'

'We do, yes. When the weather's nicer. We like the river. Or Chiswick House grounds.'

'Oh yes, I know Chiswick House. I often took you and Michelle there.'

'Did you? Wow. I didn't know that.'

'I walked around there with you on the day I was leaving London. Keeping out of the way while your grandpa packed all my clothes and your things. Sort of – one last look.'

I didn't say anything here. I picked up the empty plastic packet my oatcakes had been in and put it in my bowl.

'What a life, hey,' my mother said. 'I don't know.'

'Some life, hey,' she said.

Her hands were clenching and unclenching, just loosely, on the little glass table.

I stood and cleared our bowls away. When I came back, I leant on the back of my chair and said, 'Well at least you left him, Mum. That was brave. And you did the right thing to leave this last one, too ... I probably wouldn't get married *again* if I were you, though.' I said. I smiled then. Would she smile? Not quite, no. Instead she sort of flinched.

'I meant to ask,' I said, 'did you ever get officially divorced from Joe?'

'Oh. Well, *yes*. I am, finally. But with no help from him. It was just dreadful. So stressful. I mean, I thought the whole point in waiting was that once you're "separated" divorce is just a formality. I thought it would just be a rubber stamp, really, after five years. But no, apparently. So the papers were sent out to him twice, but he just didn't acknowledge receipt, so I didn't know what to do! I thought, oh, that's that then, is it, but then thank God Michelle volunteered to just take them round and put them in his hands. So she sort of had to ambush him, you see, and then finally, finally, things could move. I did think, for a while, oh, there's no way out! He *was* excluded from my will. Michelle helped me do that, so ... Because I did think, you know, next thing will be I die and he gets everything.'

'Were you in touch with him at all after you left?'

'Oh no. No. Not since the day I went. I mean, I did email him a couple of years ago because – well, I bought our lawnmower, you see, and the warranty on that was running out, so they sent me a notification and I *did* write an email to him then and I just said, If you want to renew the warranty on the lawnmower let me know, and he wrote back and said Fuck off and die. So.'

'Just that?'

'Mmm.'

'Goodness. Well. Let's hope that doesn't come back to haunt him, hey.'

'Mmm,' she said. 'Oh. Yes. No. Yes, let's hope!'

Back on the settee, my mother clicked on a detective show she liked called *Castle*. She'd told me about that before, in fact, how the lead actor was 'gorgeous', and she rallied now when his picture appeared.

'Oh yes. There he is! *Swoon*,' she said. 'Don't you think?'

We watched three episodes, which took care of the rest of the day.

'I just love their badinage,' my mother said.

Whenever I asked if she wanted a cup of tea she said yes, which meant she had to keep hobbling to the toilet.

'I think we need to do a cost–benefit analysis on cups of tea,' I said as she hoisted herself up for the third time with a 'One-two-three, and!'

'What do you mean?' she said.

We ordered a takeaway that night: noodles and vegetables for me, and she had the same with a bit of salmon. I poured us a glass of white wine each, and kept us topped up, and her cheeks flushed. Girlishly now, after our day together, after my shaking my head at her hoarding, after our *Castle* marathon, my mother made a shy request: she bet the lot on a bigger prize.

'*Bri-idge?*' she said, 'Don't get angry, but am I *ever* going to be allowed to meet John?'

'Oh,' I said. 'Well. We've been over that, haven't we? You and I can meet. Maybe we could walk down the river when you're better.'

'But why? Why Bridge, I don't understand.'

'Don't keep asking, Mum,' I said.

And I stood up then and cleared our takeaway boxes, then came back for our glasses.

'But why?' she said.

'Well, as I've said, I don't think it would be enjoyable,' I said. As if that was the point. We both knew she placed no value on the quality or substance of any encounter. Which was exactly why I'd never wanted one to happen.

'And, look, I don't want it,' I said. 'OK? Does that not mean anything?'

'But why?' she said, again.

'Oh, for Christ's sake. Fixate on something else, please. I don't exist to distract you. And neither does he. How's that?'

'What do you mean? What do you mean distract? It's normal for a mother to meet her daughter's boyfriend. It's normal.'

She was getting to her feet now, too; hobbling back to

the settee, where she sat, laid her crutches down, and started to cry. Those little shoulders were shaking; her mouth was turned down at the corners. I'd never seen her cry before.

'Oh Mum,' I said. 'What's all this? This isn't because you haven't met John.'

'I am,' she said, 'I *am*.'

She spoke through clenched teeth. She lifted her bad leg up onto the settee and winced.

In the kitchen, I washed my hands and then transferred the leftovers into Tupperware, ready for the fridge. I washed the glasses and dried them, and then went and sat back down in that weird dentist's armchair.

'Mum, you have to let this go.'

'You're my *daughter*,' she said.

'Ah right,' I said, 'OK.'

'It wasn't *me* who was horrible, it was your dad. It wasn't *me*.'

'Oh him. Well, you might remember that I didn't see him for a second longer than I was legally obliged to. Yet here I am.'

She looked very glum, then. She wiped her tears with the heel of her hand and then adjusted the cushions under her leg. Nothing ever held with her, did it? Nothing ever stuck. I had thought I'd been straightforward about John. Tactful, even. That's what the evasiveness had been: me being tactful; trying not to hurt her. But look where that had got us.

The stupid thing was, now it came to it, I realized I didn't much care any more if they met. What did it matter?

'But why am *I* being punished,' she said now, 'when it was *him*?'

'You're not being "punished". Don't be so weird, please. Come on. You're nearly seventy. You can't distort things like that. It's not helpful. It's not real.'

'You took John to your dad's funeral.'

'He was dead!'

'Everyone there was allowed to meet him.'

'What is this "allowed" and "punished"? You aren't a child. I'll never see any of those people again. God knows why I went. I'll bring John to your funeral, how's that?'

Here came the tears again.

'Oh for goodness' sake,' I said. 'That was a joke! I'm sorry.'

'A bad joke,' I said. But she was having her moment now. Her mouth had turned down again.

'Do you want me to tell you why, Mum?' I said. 'Why I have to keep things separate?'

She didn't answer.

'How many sentences do you think you can take on that subject? Three? Four? One? Could you consider and acknowledge one sentence?'

She didn't say anything. Her mouth was set.

For a few seconds we both sat there in our strained attitudes, her on the sofa, holding her chin up; me leaning forward in the armchair, as if thrown forward by a sudden stop.

And then the moment passed. Suddenly my mother's eyes were dry and she was frowning again; she was lifting up the piles of newspaper which surrounded her, in search of the remote. Having found that, she started scrolling through various menus on the screen.

'*Now*,' she said, 'see anything you like?'

Another night listening to next door's disco. Another early start and another hour in Nero. My mother was up when I got back, lying on the settee. She looked startled when I appeared. Her eyes were wide and wary as I handed her the paper I'd brought up.

'You OK?' I said. 'I might just read for a while. Call if you need anything! I'll stay until lunchtime today, so last call for the shops!'

I headed back to the spare room, closed the door. An hour passed. I couldn't concentrate on my book. I felt guilty and useless and bored. And the room was too hot. The pillow was too thin. The television was on very loud again, for a while, then that stopped. There was silence. Next came the tack-tack sound of her crutches on the laminate floor outside. Was she going to the bathroom?

'Bridge? Bridge?' There was a tap on the door.

'Don't open it,' I said, 'I'm coming.'

I got up, gracelessly, and slid back the door. My mother was standing out in the hallway, leaning on her crutches, with her narrow shoulders hunched.

'Come and sit with me Bridge, I'm miserable,' she said. Her mouth turned down at the corners and she started to cry again.

'OK. Sorry. Oh dear.'

She put her chin to her chest and sobbed.

'Oh dear,' I said, again. 'Would you like a hug?'

She seemed to nod, and I put my arms loosely around her and patted her back.

'Come on, let's go through.'

I followed her back into the living room and sat down and waited for her to sit, to set down her crutches and lift up her bad leg. Again I reached over and patted her shoulder with my fingers.

'What's upset you?'

'I don't know. Just . . . feel sad.'

I waited, leaning forward in the chair. Was I to say something now, or wait for her to talk?

Again I reached over and petted her shoulder.

'You feel sad,' I repeated.

She nodded.

What to do? Maybe I should I act like I had with the sorting? Roll up my sleeves and take things in hand. I tried that.

'Well, look,' I said, 'it is grim being trapped indoors for weeks, and with this nasty weather. It's bleak, isn't it? Anyone would get depressed. Never mind that you're someone who, you know, likes to keep herself busy.'

She shook her head. I'd said the wrong thing.

'Is it this place?' I said. 'Do you want to move? I'll help you this time, if you do. You could find somewhere a bit less industrial, I think. Shall we look at some property websites?'

'Oh Mum,' I said, 'don't worry!'

She was sitting sideways on the settee, with her bad leg stretched out, with her top half hunched up.

'I do *everything* you're supposed to do,' she said.

'I know,' I said.

'I don't know,' she said, 'some people just meet someone nice and that's that, isn't it?'

'Some people,' I said. I said it as if this were a point I was cautiously allowing, although, of course, I knew, I was clammily aware, that I was one of those people. I hoped that wouldn't occur to her and hurt her. I didn't think it would.

'But lots of people don't,' I said. 'That's luck, isn't it? That's just – the luck of the draw.'

'I don't think meeting someone nice is the answer,' I said.

'Besides, you can't just go out and do that, can you?' I said, taking a musing, reasonable tone now.

She didn't say anything: just sat very still.

'You have a lot on your side, you know,' I said, brightly. 'You're solvent. Independent. You have a flat and savings and a pension. A lot of women would love to be in your position,' I said. 'Without the husbands they *have* got,' I said, crassly.

She said nothing.

And again I saw that I'd got it very wrong. That it was a mean trick, suddenly to be so rational and practical in the face of her distress. It was as if I'd delicately pulled on a pair of butler's gloves. Or passed the whole thing on to a different department.

'Are you lonely?' I said. 'Is that it?'

She winced at that. Shook her head once, then rubbed

her forehead. Still, she seemed to be waiting on me. The way she was sitting there, very still, she might have been waiting for the secret of her life to be revealed at last. Or she might have been waiting for a blow. Instead, all I said was what I'd already said:

'You've had two awful husbands. You should not be aiming to get married again.'

Exactly what I'd said last night. The same larky cruelty. Cruelty dragged up as my old 'Mum, you're incorrigible!' approach.

What did I think would happen? That she might nod and smile, find it all a bit thrilling, as when I was telling her why she didn't need four black handbags? This great disowner of any feeling she expressed was owning up to something now, as best she could. But it turned out I had no way to answer her or to help.

'You *had* to get married,' she said, without looking up. And she rallied here, as insistent as she had been when I was a child, with the urgent news she could bring from 1977, that *It was just what you did*.

'I think you should have therapy, Mum,' I said.

Again she winced and slowly shook her head.

'That's something you can do if you feel stuck or frightened. You can try and find out why.'

'Are you listening, Mum?' I said. 'Can I tell you what I think? You need to think about what you want. And why what you get seems to leave you so empty. This comes up a lot with you, this note of disappointed expectation. I think you feel like a bargain has been broken when you say you do what you're supposed to do. You understand that a deal was never struck, don't you?'

'And you ought to think about why you need to be distracted so much. With loud TV and outings, and daft crushes. I understand that they are the stuff of life, that they are ways to get through life. But they seem to leave you so empty.'

This was put as clearly as I could. I had one more point, if I could say it before she bolted.

'I can't tell you how to live, Mum.' I said. 'But it does all look a bit provisional around here, doesn't it? Like you think you're going to be lifted out of all this, so it doesn't matter. Like there's something else to rush to.'

'What do you mean? I don't . . . think that.'

'I think you do.'

She shook her head, then spoke through her teeth, the tears still coming:

'I do everything you're supposed to do,' she said again. 'I go out, I "pursue my own interests", I join things, I volunteer.'

'But for what? What is it you're primed for?'

'Someone like *Castle*!' she said, crying more desperately now. 'Someone to, you know, have badinage with.'

'Oh Mum,' I said. And again I petted her shoulder.

What she said she wanted shouldn't have been out of reach, should it? Why then did I know that it was? Women her age met people. I often saw women my mother's age: women who looked like my mother, dressed like my mother, out on what looked like dates. I noticed them in cafés, or at concerts: small, neat women in their sixties. Like my mother and not like my mother. Did she see them, too? And did she feel the difference?

'Won't you think about therapy?' I said, again. 'I know you think it's for mad people, but it's helpful to have someone to talk to. *Even* for someone as sane and normal as you.' Here I smiled and leant forward to try to catch her eye. 'To get it all out, and see the patterns. You've had a tough time. Wouldn't you like someone to acknowledge that? I can show you how to find a therapist. It's dead easy.'

'Well I can look,' she said, doubtfully.

'Let's look. Can't hurt.'

'Yes. Maybe.'

'OK. Pass your laptop.'

'There are things I've never told anyone,' my mother said.

I opened her laptop. Opened the browser.

'Right,' I said.

'Things he made me do,' she said.

'Let's have a look what's available round here,' I said. 'You don't want to travel too far.'

And from there, it really was like sorting out her scarf drawer. She was mollified, she was being attended to.

'Shall we make a shortlist?' I said.

'I always think, you know, it's so long ago, why rake things up?' she said – she ventured.

'Well, because you're unhappy. They're still affecting you,' I said, stoutly.

'I think this is a good move for you. It's positive. Really brave, too. It's a better investment than being out on the tiles all the time!' I said. 'Being a gadabout!'

'Mmm,' she said.

<h1 style="text-align:center">2</h1>

On the Bayswater Road recently I saw a man who could have been my father. Or my father at forty-five, anyway. He wore a padded ski coat. He had thinning sandy hair. I found myself walking faster, for a while, to keep up with him. It gave me such a curious feeling – a stimulated feeling – closing in like that on that long stride, that bouncing hood.

I never learned anything more about the 'things he made me do'. What restraint I'd shown in not pursuing that. What sly restraint.

The next time we spoke, my mother blamed her distress on the after-effects of the anaesthetic, which were not to be discounted.

'I was full of *drugs*, Bridget,' she said, 'I'd had a *serious operation*.'

'You seemed very unhappy, that's all.'

'No I didn't. What's it to you?'

'Oh it's nothing to me,' I said. 'You've misunderstood me. I'm being conscientious. I just thought I'd see if you'd followed up with any of those therapists.'

'No,' she said.

What she *was* going to do, she told me, was go on holiday and then look into moving house.

'Oh, OK. That's good. Where will you move to?'

'Oh, I don't know. I'm just sick of this hall of residence. I want a *community*,' she said. 'So.'

'And where's the holiday?'

'Well I'm going to Cuba for Christmas. And then Thailand. And then Lisbon.'

'Good grief!' I said. And then, 'But isn't that just like what you've been doing? Only more expensive.'

'It's my money,' she said.

'It is. OK. If you think that will help.'

'What do you mean help?'

'Help you feel better.'

'I don't need to feel better. Am I not allowed to say anything?' she said. 'It's my money. Why are you so fascinated, anyway?'

'I'm not fascinated.'

'I was full of drugs *Bridget*,' she said, and then, in her sullen, obedient, teenager-made-to-say-sorry voice, she said, 'I understand that you were concerned, Bridget, and thank you for your – concern, but I was on *drugs*. I had just had a major *operation*.'

'Cool,' I said.

'Stop getting at me. Move on. A normal daughter would say Oh how interesting, Oh how brave.'

'Would she?'

'At Wine Circle they were all saying Oh how brave, we could never do what you do.'

'Were they? Because you're going on holiday?'

'I'm travelling the *world* Bridget.'

'OK!'

'Do you know many other women my age who travel on their own?'

'I want you to do what makes you happy, Mum.'

'Move on,' she said.

I had to laugh then. I said, 'Well . . .'

'Why are you so fascinated? Are you jealous, is that it?'

'I am not jealous, no,' I said.

'*Move on*,' she kept saying. She seemed to think that was a very good game. '*Move* on *move* on *move* on,' she chanted down the phone, to the tune of an old ambulance siren. Jeering at me. Jeering at the fascinated world.

3

My mother was right, though. In order to live, in order to be Hen Grant, she had to step out of a tangle of very mouldy old rope. She had to go forth, announcingly. Relentlessly and internationally.

On her way back from Portugal she passed through London. It was late summer. I met her in a pub near Euston, and on a shaded bench in the beer garden I found her full of conversation; it was quite a change.

'Well I think women talk drivel,' she said. 'I've never felt like I want to join in with women.'

'No?'

'I mean on this trip there were three men and fifteen women and I just used to sit with the men and talk to the men, so ... Ed and Andy and Dave. Oh, Dave was funny! And I said to them, oh, no, I don't want to sit with "the girls" as they called them because women, yes, just talk drivel, I think. Now Ed was a bit weird ... Just never stopped talking about his ex-wife and one lunchtime when we all sort of trooped back to the coach, Dave, who Ed had been sitting next to, said he needed that seat now to stretch his bad leg, so Ed asked if he could sit by me but you see I don't like sitting by people so just to be funny I said, oh, no, I need to stretch *my* bad leg. Anyway, Ed didn't think that was funny, and went and sat elsewhere, but then for the next week that was left of the holiday he was constantly bringing that up and sort of – getting drinks for Dave and Andy but not for me, or saving seats for them but not for me, and saying, you know, I wasn't friendly, or saying he had to stretch *his* leg now, so, yes, he was a bit weird, but Dave, and Andy, I mean Dave particularly was just so funny.'

'So was the aim to pair off, or is it just for people who don't want to be the only single person?'

'Well, yes, I think, if you don't want to be with a lot of couples or families ... It's good for widows and widowers and divorcees who don't want to go to places on their own. It's not ... I mean it's not speed dating or anything. And it's a good job, because there are always far more women than men. And the men, to be honest, can be a bit weird.'

'Do you speak to the women?'

'Yes of course. I'm not ... I'm just saying it's not me to have *girly* chats or whatever. They all want to talk about their children and I'm not interested in their children. Or their grandchildren.'

'And will you see any of them again?' I said.

'Well, Dave does live in London, so I did tell him, yes, that I'm often down visiting my *daughter*, so . . .'

'Ask him to dinner,' I said. 'In February.'

'Who?'

'This Dave character. Ask him round when you come. I mean, if you're still in touch by then.'

4

Like a plant straining towards the light, as close to the glass as a person could get, and with her head turned up as far as her position would allow her to look up, my mother stood at our living room window, waiting for Dave.

'Are you a fan of garlic, Helen?' John said.

She didn't answer. Her attention was fastened to the top of the basement steps.

'Mum?'

She looked desperate when she turned around. Torn away from her vigil.

'Yes? What?'

'I just asked if you're a fan of garlic, Helen?' John said. He was standing by the cooker. I was sitting on the settee.

Not knowing which of us to look at, my mother kept switching her eyes from one to the other. Who was the more dangerous enemy? She wasn't going to give either of us anything.

'Well ... what do you mean fan?' she said.

'I'm just putting these vegetables in. We're quite pro-garlic here, so unless you want to stay my hand, I'm going to put quite a few cloves in to do with them.'

My mother looked frozen.

This Dave, it seemed, was not a man who had accepted an invitation to dinner and would therefore be here, but rather some sort of visitant, who might at any point recede into the dim unless she was there at the window, willing him on. Forced to face us instead, she held her hands in fists by her sides.

'It's not a trick question,' I said, as mildly as I could, and avoiding John's eye then, because he might have found that impatient or mean.

She gave a tight little shrug.

'Well, I don't. Whatever. Not, you know. Just, normal amounts.'

She was frowning.

'Normal amounts! OK, I won't overdo it! And no sign of your friend yet?'

Again she shrugged, angrily, fearfully: how was she to know when we'd made her turn around?

'Well. I don't ...' she said. And then – bravely, laughing it off – 'He might have come and gone now!'

'The bell does work, Helen. I just said it might need a few goes. Are you sure you don't want to sit down? Your drink's over there.'

'No. Maybe when Dave ...'

She turned back to the window. Strange little silhouette. Awful animal attention.

From where she was standing you could see people's boots and shoes and shopping bags. You could see our bins, sitting in wet dull darkness.

John and I did exchange a look then. I turned my hands palm up. She hadn't asked him a single question. This person she'd been so desperate to meet. When John came back from putting the vegetables in he brought his glass, too, and stood by the coffee table, on which we had set out our usual pre-dinner spread for when we had guests: cashews, pickles, a bowl of topped-and-tailed radishes. He and I sipped our drinks and took handfuls of nuts or a radish or two, and ate them in the warmly lit half of the room, and regarded my mother in the unlit corner, from where she was still staring out at the basement area.

After all the fuss she'd made, all her urgent petitioning, she'd barely looked John over. I widened my eyes at him again, then, as we sat there. It was funny, in a *way*, I thought. John looked less amused. A whole evening of this before us?

It had started as soon as she'd got here. Her hello had sounded coy and false – to me, anyway. And then John had said:

'Bell worked first time, then? It's a bit dicky sometimes.'

'Oh!' she said.

What this news implied seemed to overwhelm her in the seconds that followed. She couldn't concentrate on John's questions about her journey. She said, 'Yes,' rather than really answering, and grinned and frowned unhappily, and after he took her coat she went straight to the window to wait and watch.

When Dave arrived my mother rushed out to open the door.

He appeared first from the hallway, with her close behind.

'Now can I take your *coat*?' she said, with some ceremony. 'And, yes, this is Bridget, and John. So, this is their flat, yes.'

We both stepped forward and said our hellos and shook his hand, as if we were a receiving line. Over on the rug, unintroduced, Puss was lying down and stretching. He spread his toes and yawned.

'And would you like a drink?' my mother said, as Dave handed her his coat and smiled at us. 'Or a ... *radish*, or ... *You want it, we got it*,' she said, in her Italian restaurant owner voice. 'We gotta the radishes, we gotta the nuts!' she said.

'I'll take that, shall I?' I said, lifting his coat from her arm. I took it out into the hall. When I came back in, John was still standing smiling in his kitchen nook, while my mother poured some wine for Dave. She took a glass from the cabinet, put the bottle back in the fridge.

Dave looked a bit younger than my mother. He had a nice face. Blond-ish hair. Wet eyes. He was wearing chinos and hiking shoes, and a too-small royal blue V-neck jumper over a checked shirt.

'OK!' she said, handing him the glass, before sweeping

her hand, like a magician's assistant, once more towards the snacks on the coffee table.

'And – nuts?' she said.

'Yes, I am nuts. Yes!' Dave said.

Over dinner, John asked Dave about Portugal – knowing that was where he and my mother had met. Dave was 'big into photography' he said, that was why he took those trips. He liked old buildings.

'And cats,' he said, nodding at Puss, who was back in his bed now, and asleep. 'Cats run Lisbon!' he said.

'Oh, yes!' my mother said. It was a coup that there was a cat here, when he liked cats. That was lucky. I could see her thinking that. That was a hit.

His wife liked beaches, Dave said. Not into cities. But then you could see that he was not one of nature's sun worshippers! My mother didn't react to this news, if it was news to her. She didn't flinch. Had she known? It was so hard to tell. She had told me about the photography, but was reacting to that now as if it were an enthralling revelation which she couldn't hear enough about. She looked beside herself with happiness, in fact, particularly watching Dave and John talk.

John asked her some questions next, about where she lived. This she took as a welcome cue to tell the table the story of her flat.

'Yes, I didn't know I'd moved into *student accommodation*,' she said, as if it were a funny anecdote. She said it the way one might say, 'And it turned out it wasn't a fancy dress party!'

'Yes, just lots of Chinese students,' she said. 'I want a *community*. So.'

Throughout the meal she seemed braced in anticipation for when she could speak. Which is to say, for when she could join in. That anticipation spilled over, in fact, so that she kept interrupting and interjecting. Not aggressively, but nervously, desperately. It was as if she were trying to jump onto a moving carousel. And as if John and I were trying to get through a sort of snatching storm, as she found ways to insert herself whatever the topic under discussion was, and often with a fruity or mischievous look at Dave.

Towards the end of the meal, Dave asked what John did. When John said he was an analyst, Dave was interested, and asked the questions that people often did ask. Only while John was answering, my mother interrupted, to say, in a faux whisper:

'But Dave, *Dave*, it's not for *mad* people, OK! It definitely, definitely doesn't mean you're mad. Oh *no*. Definitely not!'

I couldn't tell what Dave thought about that. He seemed a roll-with-the-punches kind of person. He'd have to be really, to have come there at all.

'Wouldn't suit me then!' he said, as I stood to clear our plates.

When I sat down again, John disappeared, and came back first with a bowl of salad, then with his cheeseboard, and finally with the biscuit barrel.

'Crackers?' he said, pulling off the lid.

Later, he described my mother as 'unyielding'. I'd pushed him for a reaction, half-frightened that he'd say he couldn't see the problem. But no, he'd seen it all right.

'I haven't come across anyone quite like that before,' he said.

He was washing up while I dried the dishes and put them away.

'I've met people who are insistent, dogmatic, aggressive, but she wasn't like that. It just quickly became obvious that she wasn't going to engage with anything that was actually being said. She had a stance, she was sticking to that, and that precluded reacting to what was actually happening. Or *experiencing* what was actually happening ... There was an absolute refusal to do that. It was disorienting. I see what you mean about that. When she appeared to react, these weren't reactions at all, were they? But her performing what she thinks she is. Or what she has decided she is. So the performance was desperately committed but gratingly false.'

'But – none of it was personal, either,' John said, squeezing out his sponge. 'It wasn't to do with *me* or *you*. She's clearly frightened of engaging. That's a sad thing. A sad and defensive thing. Here's a better way to put it, she was in an a priori reality. That's what I felt. And that reality was not going to yield to another reality.'

'The reality of reality.'

'Well, yes. Quite.'

In bed that night, I lay awake thinking about what John had said.

I found myself remembering an occasion, back in the old house, when she had had the bathroom retiled . . . There were two builders on the job: loud, dusty-faced men, singing along to Radio City. My mother was shy around them; reminded them every morning, 'Now I've put out teabags, and coffee and sugar, and there's milk in the fridge. And there are biscuits there.'

'Oh, thank you Hen. That's great.'

One night, with the job nearly done, just one wall bare, she noticed a crack on the side of the cistern, and lifting the top, saw that someone had tried to secure the damage by sticking one of the new tiles to the inside of the tank. It was pasted there with grouting. The grouting was still soft.

The next morning, she asked the older of the two men about that.

'A crack?' he said. 'Oh no. I haven't seen a crack.'

Not so friendly now. But she was still friendly. Together they went upstairs so she could show him what she'd discovered.

'Now, Hen, as far as *I'm* concerned, that was broken before we *started* this job.'

'Oh. OK,' she said. I heard her say it. I was standing by my bedroom door. She spoke happily. As if she'd been enchanted.

V

1

The Christmas lights had gone up again in town. In Soho there were shooting stars, pinned to the night, and on Piccadilly, shimmering angels. In Mayfair, huge – Cyclopean – peacock feathers swept over the wet, gilded streets.

It was a Thursday evening. I was meeting John to watch a film.

Under the Curzon marquee, I rolled my umbrella, then found my phone. There was one missed call, from Michelle. That was a jolt, to see that name, and my first thought – and the explanation I preferred – was that she must have called me by mistake. There was no message, and the call was an hour old. I turned the phone off quickly and headed inside, where John had bagged the corner table, and was sitting with his book. He wasn't looking my way, but I raised a hand to him anyway, and smiled, before heading to the bar.

We were there to watch a Polish film, from the 1980s, newly restored. I enjoyed it. The faces. The mood. It was hard to relax, though. I couldn't seem to keep one foot from jiggling.

There was no advance on Michelle's call when we got out. The next morning, too, the phone was silent.

My mother must have had her phone in her hand because she answered almost instantly.

'Oh, thank goodness,' I said, brightly. 'I had a missed call from Michelle yesterday, so I'm just checking you aren't, you know, lying in a coma somewhere! But you're obviously not, so, phew. I've been worried!'

It sounded as if she was in a café. I could hear voices. Another phone ringing.

'Can you hear me, Mum?' I said. 'Are you out and about?'

'Hello?' I said. 'Is that you, Mum?' And then, with somewhat less enthusiasm, because I didn't have time for this:

'Can you answer me, please?' I said. 'You answered the phone.'

Now came the discordant beeps of buttons being pressed, and then a voice – her voice? – said something like '*Huh*' before the line went dead.

'OK,' I said.

I went back into the kitchen, where I straightened up our two stools and moved some plates from the dryer to the cupboard.

Standing in there, by the sink, I called my mother's number again. Again, the phone was quickly answered, and again I heard sounds in the background. Only this time when I said, 'Mum. Hello,' my mother did reply.

Very slowly, and in a deep voice, she said, 'Mum.'

'Mum?' I said. 'What are you doing?'

Again, but faster this time, as if this were a game she were getting the hang of, she said, 'Mum.'

'Can you talk normally, please?' I said. 'You're frightening me.'

Now came a sort of coughed-up laugh. And very slowly, again in that slack-jawed and sarcastic-sounding mockery of a voice, she said, 'Do I.'

'OK,' I said, again, and I hung up.

'She's in Cumberland Infirmary,' Michelle told me.

'She's been in there since last Friday. She was on her way to Edinburgh with Griff, but Griff rang me to say that he didn't know what to do with her, because she wasn't speaking and her arms had gone limp. So I said, you know, *obviously*, get her to hospital. And I left work and caught the train up, but even like, on the drive from this layby they were in she deteriorated. She wet herself, she kept vomiting.'

'Oh, Christ.'

'So he did call 999 then, and Cumberland admitted her, and yeah, she's been there all week, having various tests and scans. I did ask if I should phone you but she kept saying no, not to bother you. I mean – quite insistently.'

'Right. Fair enough. OK. And you're there now, are you?'

'I am, yeah. I'm just down in the café now. I haven't been up yet.'

'Do they know what happened? What she's got?'

'They do. A brain tumour.'

'Right. Shit.'

'They'll know what kind tomorrow. I've been reading up as far as I can. There are some you can treat. There's a possibility it's benign, but from everything they're saying I think that's unlikely.'

'Right. Christ. Poor thing.'

'Yeah.'

'But she has been *compos mentis* since this happened then, if she was saying not to call me?'

'She goes in and out. It's hard to describe. What was she like with you?'

'Oh. She just copied what I said, but said it slowly. And she was pressing the buttons on her phone. And then there was this sort of unpleasant laugh.'

'Yeah. She does that. She's on steroids for the inflammation, so in theory those symptoms should be starting to calm down now. You could try and call her again if you want. She does answer her phone. It's just that she might not speak or make sense. On Wednesday she knew me and was asking why I wasn't in work. Yesterday she didn't know who I was. Or she was pretending not to know. She was calling me Grandma. And Mrs Potts. She kept saying, "Thank you Mrs Potts." I mean, have you heard of a Mrs Potts?'

'No. Never.'

'No. Me neither. I thought it might have been a teacher. Because she was doing, like, a little-girl voice.'

'Oh, great.'

'And then she thought she was at her house when she's plainly in a hospital ward. And she was telling the woman in the next bed that she'd had an aneurysm, which she hasn't. Nobody's used that word so I'm not sure where that's come from. She says "A *naneurysm*". In like, baby talk? And "A *nambulance*". She keeps saying she's "going home in a *nambulance*".'

'Jesus.'

'Yeah. Again, she's very insistent about this aneurysm. So I have explained to her a few times that she's got a brain tumour, and that it might be cancer. The consultant has told her that too. I'm just not sure it goes in. Or if it goes in it doesn't stay in.'

'No. Well. She won't want it to.'

'No, she won't.'

'Have you been up there all this time?'

'I've been coming up in the evenings, and then staying over some nights, but it is quite tough getting back if there's work. It's tiring. And my, er, partner, the man I live with, needs the car, really. So I'm not sure it's sustainable if she's going to be here much longer.'

'Has Griff been back?'

'He was supposed to be coming today but he wrote last night to say he had a migraine. Long text about that. I've heard all about how his week's going.'

'Do you need me to come then? She's likely to be there for a while yet, is she?'

'They can't tell me. I'm chasing shadows, feels like. It's a matter of getting the test results first. Or the scans. Then deciding on a treatment plan, then finding a bed for her nearer home. That is, if she's even well enough to be moved. I mean it is sod's law this happening while she was away. Or, you know, Hen's law. Makes everything ten times harder. So yeah. If you could.'

'I'm just looking up how long it takes. Carlisle is it?'

'Yeah.'

'I've got a conference this weekend. I could come Sunday evening. Then go in Monday morning. I could stay a few days. Next week is clear for me.'

'Right. You absolutely can't do Saturday?'

'No.'

'Because that's when I'm really pushed.'

'No,' I said. 'As I say.'

She left a second's silence here.

'OK,' she said. 'Well. Fine. I'll text the details. I'll give Griff another ring.'

'You think she needs someone there every day?'

'I've no idea what she needs.'

'Right.'

'I haven't spoken to her in a while,' I said. 'Did she move OK?'

'She moved in April, yeah.'

'And was that all right?'

'Seemed to be. I was round there a couple of weeks ago. She seemed fine. She was quiet.'

'Have they said how long this thing might have been in there?'

'Not yet. But, you know, with hindsight you can see maybe something was going on. She'd had trouble with her hearing, and one eye looked lazy. You think it's just age. And she was, like, getting less pleasant if I can say that. She could be quite rude. Sarcastic, like.'

'When I last spoke to her she was quiet. That was late March. I just thought she was depressed over that bloke Dave. She sent this cryptic text so I phoned her up. She answered, but she didn't say much.'

'Dave, yeah. He was – well, I don't know. I think she'd built something up in her mind there which wasn't really, you know, real.'

'No. I thought that, too. Oh dear. This is bitter.'

'Yeah. You could say that. "Bitter." OK.'

'I wondered if she was going to be finally happy when she moved. I wondered if she might settle in a bit. Did you see a lot of her?'

'Yeah, we took her out. Most Sundays. For what that was worth. But what's "finally happy" mean?'

'Oh you know. I don't know. She kept saying she wanted a community. I wondered if she mightn't make a friend who wasn't Griff, or . . . I don't know. Be less sad, I suppose.'

'"Be less sad." Huh. Well, no, she wasn't "less sad". She was putting herself about like she did in town. But it wasn't going to take, was it? The new house is nice, actually. There's a garden, and it's a nice street. When I saw it I thought OK, that's better. But she'd barely unpacked. It was just boxes. Within like, a week of being there, she was saying she wanted to go and live abroad. Move to Spain, or France. That was her new plan she said. So you say "finally happy", but I don't know what that could mean really, for her.'

'No. Of course you're right. I don't know what I meant. That was crass, I'm sorry.'

'Yeah, well.'

'Send me these details then, and I'll get up there on Sunday.'

2

My foot was twitching again, under the table in the House of Fraser Caffè Nero in Carlisle.

On Saturday the consultant had drawn the curtains around my mother's bed.

'I know it's respectful to talk to her not to me,' Michelle had told me over the phone that night, 'but Mum was just playing with her comb the whole time and reaching for the paper. She was trying to pay attention, like, but she didn't know what anything meant, so afterwards I was saying, Are you OK? and, you know, Did you understand that, Mum? But she wouldn't answer. She just wanted to do her puzzles.'

'Right.'

'It's not like they could have caught it,' Michelle said. 'If that means anything. Once it's there then it's happened.'

'Right. That does help, actually.'

'So now she has to decide if she wants treatment.'

'Like what?'

'An operation. Chemo. Radiotherapy. With all three you might get an extra few months. So. I'm not sure how she's supposed to decide. You know, this person who thinks I'm her mother and that she's still married to Joe. But we're going to have to try to explain.'

'Did she react at all?'

'Not really. She was just humming. Maybe that was the reaction. I tried to give her a hug but she just stayed still. You'll have to try on Monday. She needs to know.'

I finished my coffee and queued for another one. There was a *Times* on the next-door table, so I looked through that for a while, and then texted John. Michelle said my mother didn't come round until midday. I didn't much fancy going back to the hotel, so, noticing that my nails were looking a bit ragged, I googled nail salons instead, and called one, then followed the map on my screen to a ten o'clock appointment.

The young woman who was seeing to me said, 'Day off?'

'Oh no,' I said, 'sadly not.'

And as she dunked my right hand into the plastic hand-shaped basin and set to filing the nails on my left hand, I told her about my mother. The collapse on the motorway. The decision to be made about treatment.

'Ah, bless her,' the young woman said.

'Yeah,' I said.

Pulling on my coat at the till, I came back to the subject.

'When you think,' I said, 'of all the people who'd really *deserve* a brain tumour! I mean, richly deserve one!'

'I can think of a few!' she said.

Next my phone-map took me through the wet and windy decked-out streets to the bus stop by the station, from where, Michelle had told me, I was to get the number 60 up to the hospital. She'd also said, and then reminded me in a text message, that I should make sure to take in a *Guardian* and a pen, because our mother tended to lose hers, and some Ginger Nut biscuits, and Nivea hand cream. I had all of these, but in the hospital atrium, still with time to kill, I had a drift around the Londis and the Smiths. There was a café, too, and I got in the queue there.

As I paid for my coffee, somebody called my name.

'Bridge!' said the voice.

'Bridge! Here!'

It was Griff, hailing me from the far corner, where he was half standing up at his table. I lifted my hand hello, and went over.

'Hello!' I said.

'Hi Bridge,' he said, clearing his bags from the other seat.

'Just some provisions,' he said, 'for her ladyship.'

He'd done a run to Boots, he told me. Got some wet wipes and hand cream. And he'd brought her some Ginger Nut biscuits.

'Ah great,' I said, 'and I've got her paper ...'

'Oh, Bridge, isn't it terrible?' he said. 'I can't take it in!'

'It is,' I said.

'Shelley told me I might see you.'

'Were you here yesterday?' I said.

'Well. I was meant to be. But the whole weekend was a write-off, I'm afraid, so Shelley did do an extra day. I just – I get these splitting heads, Bridge, and I don't know if it's being stressed or being in shock brought it on, but I was just laid up. And even when they ease off I'm wiped out for days. So I just – I couldn't think, Bridge. I thought if I get in that car I'll end up in the hospital myself!'

He told me about his charity shop shifts and his volunteering schedule; how he'd managed to move things around so he was free today.

'I probably needed another day in bed, to be honest, but I just couldn't stay at home, knowing she was here.'

I broke my flapjack up and asked if he wanted some.

'Oh thanks, yeah, go on,' he said.

'I can't get over how *fast* this happened,' he said. 'Talk about out of the blue.'

'Mmm,' I said.

'I'd noticed she was quiet, Bridge,' he said, 'the last few times I'd seen her. But I thought it was me. I thought I must have done something to upset her, because she was being quite short with me. On the phone. She seemed very distracted. She'd just keep sighing and not, like, answering me.'

I thought – I didn't say – that she might have been cross with him as well. They were each other's closest friends, but my mother often didn't much like Griff. She was grateful for him sometimes. Sometimes, especially these last few years, she had such a sullen look when I asked about him, as if it were just one more humiliation for him to be what she'd got.

'But then,' he said, 'I mean, I've told Michelle this too, but I know that's always been her way of coping, you see, when she's had an upset. Just – shutting down. So I did wonder if there hadn't been some kind of disappointment. When she was stressed or unhappy, she would always just go to bed for a few days and make herself sleep. She *always* said that,' he said – emphatically, as if I were about to disagree, 'that if she could just sleep for a day, or two days, just block everything out *totally*, then that was it, she'd be fine.

'So I wasn't sure if it was just that, but I was *slightly* concerned, because as I say, it went on for a few weeks. She just wasn't saying much at all. Monosyllables. And very flat? Her voice just sounded flat. I even thought Alzheimer's, maybe? Beginnings of. I was going to see how she was on this trip and then decide if I needed to get in touch with Shelley.

'As I say though, she seemed fine when I picked her up. She was all packed and waiting for me. I mean, waiting out on the kerb with her weekend bag. The only thing was, she wanted the car radio on very loud. She kept turning it up when I'd turned it down. Every time I said it was too much her hand just reached out and put it up to the maximum. And that *wasn't* like Hen.'

'No,' I said. Although, of course, it *was* quite like her, wasn't it? I remembered the television getting louder in the wake of my looking in on her when I was small.

'Then, as you know, it all just went. She started retching.

She couldn't speak. So the next nightmare was trying to find Shelley's number.'

He told me how he'd had to turn around and come *back* to the hospital, that first day – he was halfway home when he realized he'd driven off with her suitcase!

'All her things!' he said.

'In the trade we call that a cock-up!' he said.

My mother was on the third floor. At midday we headed up. We stood together in a huge lift. We pressed buttons to open doors, and moved forward into thicker, stiller air, ready to smile when we turned this corner? No, the next.

'Here she is!' said Griff.

Her bed was at the end of the bay, by the window. She was sitting, on top of the covers, in her own clothes: a T-shirt and leggings. She was kneeling on the covers, in fact, and when she saw us, she beamed at us. Kneeling and beaming, she looked like a child in a Victorian print, on Christmas morning, excited by snowfall.

'I'm back!' said Griff.

'Hello Mum!' I said, and I leant in and gave her a hug, as best I could manage. She didn't say anything. Didn't seem able to. Her eyes were wide and her lips were pursed. Her mouth was a small diamond.

I pulled around a chair and sat down. Griff did the same, by the window. He started piling out all the loot he'd brought, onto the bed. The biscuits. The cotton wool balls. My mother clasped her hands together. She said, 'Ooh!'

I added my own bounty – the newspaper and the pen –
and she leant forward to take them first. As she did so, I saw
something was bulky under her leggings. She was wearing a
nappy.

'I was just telling Bridge about our adventure,' Griff said,
'on the M6.'

'I thought you were in a mood with me, didn't I? You were
so quiet!'

My mother shook her head at me. All incredulity. In a
mood with *Griff*? She seemed to be saying.

'And naturally it was raining, wasn't it? So you were dashing through the storm, weren't you, in the ambulance, with
the siren going.'

'Can you understand us OK, Mum?' I said. 'You look like
you can!'

She nodded and said, 'Yes. Yes. Just . . .'

Here she waved her hands.

'You lose your words?'

She nodded again. Eyes wide. She looked exhilarated.

At two o'clock a nurse came through the ward with the
dinner menus. Griff read out the choices and my mother
said, 'Coo!' and she pointed at what she wanted. Griff said,
'I'm jealous!' about the pudding and my mother seemed
tickled, pleased.

We didn't speak to her about her diagnosis. At six o' clock
we left.

*

The next day, the Tuesday, when I was on my own with her, I tried the same tack. I read out the dinner choices like Griff had done. I tried to use her newspaper, too, to talk to her. 'Isn't this dreadful?' I said, about a headline, or 'Do you know who that is?' about a picture of a soap star. I read out a Quick Crossword clue and she tried to answer. Or rather – as in a game of charades – she would communicate that she knew the answer, and then it was down to me to make suggestions, and for her to shake her head and frown, or nod and urge me on, until I guessed it right. If she let me know that she was drawing a blank then it was me who did the mimes and the gurning, until she said, 'Oh! Oh!' to let me know she'd got it. There were some words she could say. Sometimes what she said was adjacent to what she meant. She said 'yellow' for lemon and 'big *doors*' for wardrobe. She couldn't manage more than three or four words at a time.

There were associations, too, I found. I said something like, 'It was filthy weather yesterday, wasn't it?' and she sang, 'Yesterday', as in the song, and smiled eagerly, knowing that this, too, was an answer she'd got right. Or if I mentioned Michelle she immediately sang 'Michelle', as in that Beatles song. I told her that Griff had been in touch with her neighbours and asked them to push the mail through, and she sang the word 'Neighbours', as in the Australian soap. So the afternoon passed, with me in my daytime TV presenter guise again: making sure to enjoy everything she said. Giving exaggerated reactions.

*

182

There were five beds in the bay. Five women. Mounted at the head of every bed was a whiteboard, with slots for the patient's name and the consultant's name, and then there was a box headed, What matters to me. Opposite my mother, what mattered to Eileen was 'Getting Home'. And in the bed next to hers, Linda wanted 'A nice <u>Cuppa</u>' – this clarified in a different handwriting – 'OF TEA'. My mother's board said 'dignity'. I'd spotted that when I came in with Griff and wondered about it. She couldn't have said that, could she? The dreadful state she'd been in when she arrived. So had it been Michelle, or Griff? Maybe 'dignity' was what they wrote when someone was so poorly their dignity was at hourly risk. Meanly, I even wondered if dignity was nurses' code for her being stuck-up, which she wasn't, but she might have seemed that way, with her shrugs and her silences. I'd seen how she was with the nurses. Not meeting their eye when they changed her sheets. She just turned away and pointed at the mess. I said thank you but my mother didn't. It was unfair to notice that. My mother had a brain tumour. But I did notice.

On the four afternoons I spent there that week, Eileen had no visitors. She slept after lunch. Later she sat up reading, one of those north country romances. The girl on the cover wore a shawl, and had windblown hair and ruddy cheeks. On Wednesday, the second day I was in there alone with my mother, I asked Eileen if she minded if I opened the window.

'No, go on!'

'You won't be too cold?'

'That's fresh air pet, not cold. Need all I can get of that!'

It was this exchange that provoked my mother's first full sentence.

'No one asked *me*,' she said. Although I had asked her. I'd asked her seconds ago, and she hadn't answered, she'd just kept turning the pages of the *G2*.

Eileen was very old. Her hair was a bit of fluff, and her bony hands were the colour of candlewax. Going to the bathroom, she used a Zimmer frame, and had to rest after every step.

That day, I found myself watching her pushing on, hunched over her frame.

'How are you doing, love?' asked the nurse who was bending over her. 'Not far now.'

Eileen said, 'Oh. I'm struggling, pet.'

I realized my mother was watching this, too, when she said, through her teeth, and in a voice that was a high-pitched alarm:

'If I ever *get like that*.'

'What's that?' I said.

'If I ever get like that!' she said again, chuckling. She didn't finish the thought, but here I knew it was not a case of her losing her words. Since I was small, my mother had only ever voiced the first half of that proposition. If ever we had seen anyone particularly unfortunate – old or ill, or mad – on the television, or out and about, she had said, 'If I ever get like that!' leaving the second half understood.

Here was the odd thing, though. Topsy-turvy-wise, now, as

Eileen stopped again and shook her head, my mother did say what she never had. She said, *'Just kill me.'* Almost laughing again, she said, 'Just kill me, *if I ever get like that!'*

On Thursday, I arrived at two. I gave my mother her *Guardian*, and she turned the pages slowly. She frowned, and pretended to read. As when I was small, she didn't like letting go of her newspapers, and a good stack of them had built up on her bedside unit. I'd taken a couple away with me last night, and on the bus back into town had looked at the answers she'd managed to fill in for herself, in the Quick Crossword, and in the sudoku. They were the right answers. So something was working in there. Outwith that persistent little engine, though . . . when I spoke to her, she still often didn't respond or even register that she was being spoken to. That gave me an evil licence, sometimes. I could find myself carrying on these mad monologues, as a child might with a toy. What strikes me now is that this perhaps wasn't so different from the way I'd always spoken to her. Which is to say, assuming half of what I said wouldn't 'go in', or if it did, would not be understood, and would be rudely sent back, with a 'What's that mean?' or a 'Why?'

'It's boring this, isn't it?' I said now, smiling, as if I'd said, 'Isn't this great?'

'You know we're still waiting to hear when you can get home,' I said. 'Or not home-home, but to a bed *near* home. We should hear soon.'

'Mmm,' she said.

'Do you remember, you're going in an ambulance?' I said. 'We're in Carlisle now.'

She huffed at that.

I said, 'Do you remember?'

'Oh some hope,' she said, finally. This apparently in response to one of her own thoughts, rather than to anything I'd said.

Something had shifted that day. She was agitated. Her right hand kept tapping on the bedsheet.

'Mum,' I said, leaning forward to try and catch her eye. 'Can I talk to you?'

There was no response.

I asked again, and now she frowned and said:

'Yes if you want.'

But she didn't look up from her newspaper.

'OK. Do you know what's happened to you?' I said. 'Do you remember what the consultant said?'

'Hmm …' she said, performing a frown. It was as if I'd just read out one of her crossword clues. As if she were about to say, 'Ask me another!'

'Well, I'll tell you,' I said. I put my hand on her right hand now, which she didn't like. She flinched. She wanted to keep tapping.

'OK,' I said, taking my hand back.

'You have a brain tumour,' I said. 'Just here,' I said, and I touched her then, just above her right eye. 'It is cancer,' I said.

Here she pulled a sort of 'scared' face.

I went on, 'That's why you collapsed. That's why you've had

trouble hearing. They can treat it to give you some extra time, but it is terminal. Do you understand? It's called a glioblastoma. They can't cure it. They can't remove it.'

Her eyes were moving. But it was as if she'd spotted something over my shoulder: some other call on her attention.

'I'm so sorry, Mum,' I said. But there was no response. Now she was turning her head to frown at her bedside unit.

Her sponge bag was there and she reached for that. It was a purple cotton bag with a drawstring. Having pushed her newspaper away, she emptied the bag onto the bed, and started going through its contents. She took her little plastic comb, and then her tweezers and her face powder. All packed for her weekend away with Griff. She laid them out in a row.

I took the bag and shook out what was left in there. A lot of scrunched tissues. A couple of dusty cotton buds.

'Oh dear. This needs a sort-out, doesn't it?' I said. 'Shall I throw these away?'

When I got back from the bin she was sitting on the edge of the bed. When I sat next to her, she stood up and stepped over to the window. Yesterday, she'd stood there for a good half an hour, watching the ambulances arrive. I'd stood with her and she had said, 'Uh-oh,' as we'd both watched somebody get stretchered in.

Now, trying to get back into that spirit, I said, 'Is someone in trouble, Mum?'

No answer. So I stood up and went to the window.

There was no action on the forecourt now. Instead my mother pointed at one of the parked ambulances.

'Look Bridge,' she said.

'Scottish Ambulance Service,' she said, or rather, carefully read out.

'Oh, yes,' I said. 'If only I had my *I Spy* book. *I Spy at the Hospital*. Imagine that.'

I don't know why I said that. Perhaps because I knew she would have liked imagining a book like that, before she was ill. Now she just came and stood closer to me. She pulled that scared face again.

On Friday, when I got in, her bed needed changing. 'Press the button, Mum,' I said, but she didn't want to. She said, 'Stop *bullying* me.'

Her right hand would not stop tapping on the sheet.

She didn't care about the newspaper now. Her attention was fixed on the end of the bay: where the consultant would appear.

Under her breath, repeatingly, my mother said, 'Bored now.' Through her teeth, in her American voice, she said, 'Let's get this show on the road!' And then, 'Let's get this road on the show, hey!'

This was entirely my fault. I'd said again that the consultant would be along 'soon' with news of when she could go. Now she was expecting him every minute. Now that moment was all there was.

I tried to bring her attention back to the newspaper, to the puzzles. She frowned and shook her head. Again she said, 'Stop *bullying* me.'

'I think I'll go downstairs for a sandwich,' I said. 'Do you want anything?' I said, as I put my handbag over my shoulder.

This time, when I came back, I found my mother had packed most of her things away. The sponge bag was gone: back in her weekend bag, I presumed, which was all zipped up by her bedside unit. The old newspapers were in a neat pile. She'd got dressed in her outdoor clothes and was sitting on the edge of the bed. She hadn't put her boots on but had put them out ready, next to her dangling feet.

At about four o'clock, with no sign of the consultant, I managed to persuade her to take off her coat and lie down again. I found her paper and gave her a pen, and when she seemed absorbed in her sudoku, I said:

'I have to go back to London today. I think Michelle can be here on Sunday. There might be some movement on where you're headed by then!'

She didn't react to this. I couldn't tell if she could hear me or understand me.

'Do you think you'll be OK for a day on your own?' I said.

I'm not sure why I asked that, because there was nothing anyone could do about it. It was a day no one could cover.

'I could speak to Griff and see if he could come up,' I said. (Which was stupid, too, and a lie. I knew he was working.)

'Ugh,' she said. 'No. Not Griff.'

'OK, just an idea!' I said. 'He'll be at one of his jobs, anyway, I expect. He keeps busy, doesn't he?'

She sighed at that.

'Oh yes very busy,' she said, under her breath.

'Well, you'll have a day to yourself then,' I said.

'Thank God for *that*,' she said, again quietly, to herself, or as an aside.

'You don't want visitors?' I said. 'Gosh. I wish I'd known that before I spent four days sitting here, bored out of my mind. I'd love to go home now, actually. But I've told Michelle I'll stay till six.'

My mother was frowning at her *Guardian* now; flipping through the pages; pretending to read.

'Are you bored with my company?' I said, brightly. Luring her on. And she was lured on.

'Yes,' she said. And in what I think was her old Katharine Hepburn voice, she said, 'You bore me now. Go!'

'Ah!' I said. 'Really?'

'Yes. *Go*. Leave me now,' she said, swiping the air imperiously.

'You won't feel abandoned?'

'I am completely indifferent,' she said, looking past me again, to the end of the bay.

'Are you joking?' I said. And looking directly at me this time, she repeated herself, speaking through her teeth:

'I am completely indifferent as to whether I have visitors.'

'So we've all been wasting our time. Damn. Maybe I should tell Michelle not to bother, then. That'll save her some time. Money, too. It's very expensive, getting up here. And then there's the hotel.'

'So that's good to know,' I said, 'for future reference.'

She was back to her paper now, though; flicking through that contentedly.

3

First came a 'debulking' operation. But the tumour quickly started to grow back.

Michelle took her in. She and her partner set up a bedroom in their living room. They had to hoist her into the bath; hoist her on and off the toilet. Michelle drove her to her radiotherapy sessions.

Some days, she wouldn't speak to Michelle. She pointed at what needed doing.

'She's furious,' Michelle said. 'You can feel it coming off her.'

While Michelle looked for permanent residential care for her, they decided to see if she could cope back in her own house, with help coming in three times a day. She needed to be changed and fed. She had to take her chemotherapy pills, and various other pills. Anti-nausea pills. Painkillers. Michelle went there every day. She took her to her appointments and did her shopping. She made the house safe, and bought any equipment she needed.

Even so, the situation could never quite be contained. One morning a carer arrived to find our mother on the phone, giving her bank details to someone claiming they could invest in Bitcoin for her; another day Michelle found my mother had blocked the toilet by using it as a bin-cum-laundry basket: stuffing her pads and her soiled leggings down there.

Michelle had bought her a lanyard so she could wear her phone around her neck, and her panic button. My mother sometimes answered when I called. But then I'd often just hear her pressing the buttons before the line went dead. If I managed to snag her attention, I'd ask how she was. To that she would either say, 'Bit livelier,' or, 'Bit wobbly on my feet.' These phrases, evidently, were easy to retrieve. Otherwise, there was often only her strange coughed-up laugh, or a tight-sounding, 'Mmm.'

'Are you getting any rest?'

'Mmm.'

'Has Michelle been yet?'

'Mmm. You'd think!'

'She has or she hasn't?'

'Oh yes!'

'What's that mean?'

*

She was back in her new house for three weeks. I visited twice. The first time was a Saturday. I arrived with shopping and found my mother sitting in the middle of the settee, leaning forward to frown at a very loud television. Her right hand was glued to the remote. She glared at me when I spoke, and when I asked if anything needed doing she said, 'Hoovering.'

When the carer arrived, I went out. I sat for an hour in a Costa Coffee next to an Asda.

As I keyed in the code to let myself back in, I could hear the television, even louder than before.

'What's this?' I said, brightly, as I sat down.

'Documentary about the A1.'

'Ah, great.'

'Could it be a tiny bit quieter?' I said.

No answer.

'Mum?' I said.

'That's really loud Mum. Please turn it down. I can't think.'

'Get some earplugs,' she said, and that was the last thing I got out of her that day.

But then, why was I thinking about getting anything out of her?

I went back the following weekend. This time, she was asleep on the settee. I muted the television and sat there looking at the paper. There were some breakfast things in the washing-up bowl, so I washed them: a cereal bowl and a mug. I went up to her bedroom and made the bed, and straightened out the things on her dressing table.

All the while, Michelle was visiting homes, and working out how to cover the costs, and then waiting for a place for our mother. At last there was somewhere available. I asked if I could go with them when she moved.

On the day, Michelle picked me up at Piccadilly. From there we drove to our mother's house, where Griff was getting her ready. He wheeled her out to us, then went back for her suitcases.

I got out and helped to fold her wheelchair, then stood back while Michelle fitted it in the boot with the bags.

Griff sat in the front, my mother in the back with me.

I looked out of my window for most of the forty-minute drive.

In the reception area of the Elms, and then in her new room, my mother looked around wide-eyed. All interest. It reminded me of when John and I brought Puss home from the shelter: when he stepped cautiously out of his travel cage. My mother, too, peered silently around, and looked up, as if taking each room's dimensions.

She still had that restless right hand. It tapped her leg, as if repeating a code, or she would touch her forehead, where her scar was, or, missing that spot, would swipe at the air in front of the scar.

Michelle had already been in with some things to brighten

up her room: a new blanket, a pot of geraniums. There were no pictures – my mother had never had pictures on her walls – and no photographs. Instead Michelle had brought various cards she had been sent. Some were recent, some from when she'd had that knee operation. There were even some old birthday cards. Michelle had arranged them on the windowsill and on the chest of drawers and the bedside unit.

When Michelle said, 'This seems all right, doesn't it?' and when I said, 'Nice big telly there, Mum,' our mother did not respond. She did not seem to hear us. She did attend to certain sounds from down the corridor.

One thing moved her to speak. That was when, an hour or so later, the nurse wheeled her back to reception with us as we were leaving. Behind the desk was a crowded noticeboard, with taxi numbers, and rosters, and a few colourful Thank You cards. In among all of that was an Order of Service; partially hidden, but it was clear what it was: there was the photograph; there were the dates. My mother's right hand went to that. She pointed from her chair. Michelle crouched to ask her what she'd spotted, and she chuckled and said:

'They don't call it the departure lounge for nothing!'

At her funeral, when the celebrant told my mother's life story, she did not use my father's name. That would have been at Michelle's instruction and it seemed right to me. Instead, when it came to it, she said that there had been a marriage, and two daughters, and that 'this marriage, sadly, was a very difficult time for Helen'.

'But Helen – or *Hen*, yes' – this with a nod to Griff – 'was nothing if not resilient,' she went on.

Later she said:

'Nothing about Hen could ever be described as ordinary.'

And: 'Hen used to say she had FOMO' – a pause here – 'which some of you, the younger people here, will know is "Fear Of Missing Out".'

Various things in that line.

At one point she said, 'Hen never lost her sense of humour.'

My mother was in the care home for six weeks. The last time I saw her, we spent a couple of hours in her room, watching television. Or anyway, the television was on. I clicked through the channels, while she sat up in her armchair. At first, with that restless right hand, she was fiddling with the hem of her T-shirt. Then she started touching her scar.

'Bit of *Columbo*?' I said.

'Do you remember his catchphrase?' I said.

Columbo stood in a rich woman's living room, with his arms clasped about himself, and then he frowned with his hand at his forehead. It seemed my mother did remember, though she couldn't say it herself. She seemed to respond when I said it; when I did the voice, and frowned. When I tapped my forehead, as he did; as she was doing now, for her own reasons.

I replied to my emails while we sat there. When my mother made a moaning sound, I gave her her juice beaker, and helped her hold it up to her mouth. I sat for a while with my hand on her left hand.

As I was getting my coat on, at six o'clock, one of the burlier carers came in, pushing the hoist.

'It's that time again, Hen!' he said.

'Well. Bye then, Mum,' I said, again holding then squeezing her limp left hand. I put my lips to her hot head, then leant down to perform a hug. I held her loosely, around those narrow shoulders, and then squeezed a bit harder. As I stepped back, the carer set to strapping her into the sling. He passed the fabric behind her, then under her legs.

Another carer, a young woman, had come in to help with the transfer. She picked up my mother's beaker from the bedside table to check she didn't need a refill. I stood in the doorway, out of their way.

The man pressed a button and my mother was hoisted slowly, until she was suspended some three feet above her chair. She was slumped forward. Her face was set.

No scattered, sunlit crowd. No ancestral landscape, or deafening din of helicopter blades.

Now she hung there, as if she were being weighed. Now the machine's arm swung. My mother was lowered onto the bed. The man unclipped the sling and folded it away. The woman lifted my mother's legs together, laid them out and pulled up the sheet.

Acknowledgements

The author would like to thank Arts Council England and the Society of Authors for grants that supported the completion of this book. She is also grateful to the Royal Literary Fund for a Fellowship.